GYRFALCON

Gyrfalcon n. (*pron.* jire-falcon), also gerfalcon. *Falco rusticolus.* A large falcon of cold northern regions.

Grace Wells

Grace lives with her two children high up on the side of Sliabh na mBan in County Tipperary, a long way from London where she grew up. On leaving school she worked in the film and television industry, eventually becoming a freelance producer. In 1991 she came to Ireland with the intention of devoting more time to writing. An unmapped path through organic gardening, motherhood and work facilitating biography and poetry workshops for people with special needs ultimately brought her to *Gyrfalcon*, her first book. She teaches creative writing and is the Literature Officer for South Tipperary Arts Centre.

GYRFALCON

Grace Wells

THE O'BRIEN PRESS
DUBLIN

First published 2002 by The O'Brien Press Ltd,
20 Victoria Road, Dublin 6, Ireland.
Tel: +353 1 4923333; Fax: +353 1 4922777
E-mail: books@obrien.ie
Website: www.obrien.ie
Reprinted 2002.

ISBN: 0-86278-765-3

British Library Cataloguing-in-Publication Data
Wells, Grace
Gyrfalcon
1.Finn MacCumhaill, 3rd cent. - Juvenile fiction
2.Children's stories 3.Fantasy fiction
I.Title
823.9'2[J]

2 3 4 5 6 07
02 03 04 05 06 07

The O'Brien Press receives
assistance from

Editing, typesetting, layout and design: The O'Brien Press Ltd
Interior illustrations: Anne O'Hara
Printing: Cox & Wyman Ltd

CONTENTS

Acknowledgements

There were a lot of people who helped bring this book into being. First, thanks must go to my children, Sliabh and Holly, and to my family in England. Yet this book belongs much more to Ireland and to the vibrant community of the Tipperary/Kilkenny region. There are countless people I know here whose ability to 'stand' for things was essential to my own life and to my perseverance with the more lofty ideas in this book. Amongst others, I'd like to particularly thank Kerry Hardie, Elinor Mountain, Mary Kavanagh, Judith Ashton, Bill McCullom, Peter Binder, Ian Wright & David Grant. Also an immeasurable degree of gratitude goes out to all the special people I know in the Camphill communities, most particularly to Gladys and Patrick Lydon who continue to harbour me. My thanks also go to the artistic community of Clonmel, particularly Mary O'Gorman, Miriam & Al Robinson, Brendan Maher, Des Shortt (who arrived most serendipitously on the right day to tap my compass and show me it no longer showed true north) and, above all, to my darling Stephanie Horton.

I am aware that *Gyrfalcon*'s flight to publication was only so swift and sure because of the kindness of Fergus and Maireád FitzGerald. The O'Brien Press was a fundamental part of the book's progress and beauty, and the sensitivity and wisdom of Íde ní Laoghaire, Emma Byrne and particularly Rachel Pierce are here throughout.

Much of the essence of *Gyrfalcon* came from the forces of Sliabh na mBan itself, but the novel is also deeply informed by the inspirational work of John Moriarty.

Last thanks must go to this book's five midwives who held and supported me throughout the fun times and the dark times of its making. They each saved my life on more occasions than I care to remember, but rest assured Libby Grant, midwife of common sense, Eliza Dear, midwife of writing, Amy King, midwife of publication, Sue Walker, midwife of practicality, Silvia Tilly, midwife of the soul, I do remember each and every one of them.

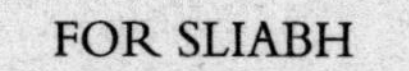

FOR SLIABH

'There is a secret medicine
given only to those who hurt so hard
they can't hope.'

Rumi
(1207–1273)

Chapter One

THE SPECIAL PLACE

Gyr darted back and crouched in against the low wall. There was definitely somebody up there ahead of him, moving about behind the overgrown hedge. He frowned. Whoever it was stood between him and his special place. Gyr listened carefully and a thin smile flickered across his lips. He could hear an angry growl of muttered complaints. Old Mahoney. It had to be him.

As Gyr listened, his attention wandered from the gravelly human voice to the more powerful music of the waterfall that called to him from his secret ravine. For months, Gyr had heard that sound and thought it was just the stream, the Lingaun, which ran from the windswept mountain slopes high above their house down through the townland of Glenaskeogh and on to the comforting village that nestled far below in the valley. But now Gyr knew it wasn't just the stream, it was a waterfall, tumbling into a hidden ravine that he had claimed as his own.

What was Old Mahoney doing behind the hedge anyway? Checking on his brambles the way most farmers check their sheep? Gyr moved his body into a low squat and leaned into the wall. His tensed shoulders dropped and relaxed and he breathed out a long white plume of misted breath into the cold January air. This was the only trouble with his special place: it had such good natural defences it made it hard to get there. Gyr grinned, he wondered if you could call a grumpy neighbour like Mahoney a natural defence.

Usually people spoke of things, like forts, as having the natural defence of a hill, or a river, or a steep cliff. His special place had loads of natural defences, for a start it was tucked into the mountain between Old Mahoney's and Bradshaws's land, so it was almost invisible, as if it were in another world altogether. If you didn't already know it was there, you might never find it. Then it also had the advantage of the Lingaun running right through it, which acted as a deterrent but also as a shield because if you did actually take the time and trouble to trek all the way up from the village through the water, you probably could get to the special place without leaving a trail or a scent behind you. But then, who was going to tramp through icy waters just to follow a stream?

The easiest way into the ravine was to fight through the gorse and brambles of Old Mahoney's land, but unless you were very determined you'd probably give up that idea for a bad lot. The only other entrance – and this was the way Gyr had taken that first day two weeks ago when he had accidentally come across the place – was through the narrow drainpipe that channelled the Lingaun under the mountain road. The ravine was certainly tricky enough to get to without having the extra possibility of stepping onto the landmine of Old Mahoney's explosive temper. What if the old man did actually explode at you? Gyr wondered. He suppressed a snigger. A scary thought: he didn't want to chance it.

'Gyr!'

A small reedy voice called his name.

'Gyr!'

He stuck his head up over the wall and looked back up through the Gate Field towards home. He scanned the pale-green grass and the stony track that led through it. He saw the cows huddled over by the red haybarn in the corner up near the house, and he saw a small, blue-clad figure halfway up the far gate: Poppy.

'Blast!' Gyr grumbled to himself. Poppy certainly wasn't a natural defence. She was more like a secret weapon, especially if you put her on the tin whistle!

'Gyr! Where are you?' Her voice carried shrilly on the frosted air. Gyr hoped she'd just go away. He doubted she would brave it down through the cows; however much he reassured her they were harmless, she stayed afraid of them. And even if she did make it through the field, the presence of Old Mahoney would have her running back up to Mum, unless, of course, she found Gyr first. This was it, Gyr would have to move now, before either Poppy found him or Old Mahoney appeared shaking his angry head. There was nothing else for it except the drainpipe.

Crouching down, almost on all fours, Gyr sprinted across the mountain road and threw himself towards the stream bank. He felt excited and slightly silly – it was childish, hiding from his little sister. But it was his special place after all, and it was his secret. He dived head first into the concrete drainpipe, icy water splashing up at him, and he curled his body into a tight ball to keep as dry as possible. He moved into the narrow pipe an inch at a time until he was about halfway through.

I must be right in under the road now, he thought.

Gyr stopped to listen. No sound of Old Mahoney, or Poppy, only the stream water coursing through the pipe and the roar of it falling over the waterfall as it came out the other end, into his ravine.

Gyr hunched himself up in the small dark space and rested his chin on his wet knees. For a minute he felt guilty that he was keeping his special place a secret, but he had his own reasons. Back in August, when they had first come to Glenaskeogh, Gyr had done all his exploring with Dad. Together they'd found the reservoir for skimming stones and together they'd discovered the best hiding places. Gyr wanted to show his special place to Dad first. Mum and Poppy would have to wait until after Dad came back from England. After that, Gyr would show it to everybody, including his new friend Luke.

Gyr knew he wasn't really being fair to Poppy. If she stopped her rhyming and her whining, she could be good fun, and he knew they could have some great adventures together in the ravine, if he did show it to her. Above all he knew his mother would love the place. She would think it beautiful and say it was magical. But all too soon she would be making Gyr tread carefully and whisper, so as not to disturb the fairies. Before he knew it, she'd be up to something daft like taking photographs of Poppy in a white dress and a pair of wings. Stuff fairies, Gyr thought. The hidden ravine was a place where rebels and wanted men had hidden for months on end, a place where pirates had stashed their treasure, where the legendary Finn MacCumhail and his warriors, the Fianna, had punished traitors.

That was the trouble with Mum, Gyr thought as the stream water began to soak through to his socks, she was always going on about fairies and angels and goddesses. She was always burning incense and meditating, joining spiritual groups and going to hear gurus. The worst of it was the chanting she and Poppy were into whenever they went anywhere in the car. Gyr refused to do it. He knew it upset his mother, but in some way he wanted to upset her. Mum just said he was being judgemental and shouldn't dismiss something he had never tried, but no way was he going to try something that stupid. 'The Earth is our Mother, we must look after her,' Mum and Poppy would sing, over and over. Gyr could almost hear it now, resonating off the concrete walls of the drainpipe. The insistent, relentless cheerfulness of the chant drove Gyr mad. He hated the way it broke into, 'Heya Nona, Hoa Nona'. Of all the ridiculous lines in the world! They sang those lines four times, then 'The Earth is our Mother' again, but the last line changed to, 'She will look after us'. Mum and Poppy always got it wrong. They never counted to four properly and they always got the lines mixed up, which only made them laugh and start again. Every time they did it, Gyr's ears burned and he would stare out of the window, wishing he were somewhere, anywhere else.

It wasn't so bad when they lived in London. The city was full of people into different things, people wore funny clothes all the time, there were so many different ways of life and religions that nobody much cared or noticed what anyone else was doing. Here there was only one religion and people didn't even know what a guru was.

'Thankfully!' Gyr whispered and huddled into himself.

The icy water was beginning to soak further into his

clothes, but he wanted to stay there, in the small, dark space beneath the road. He didn't want to move and be reminded of where they lived beneath the wild empty mountain. He didn't want to think of their few, scattered neighbours who were farmers, or the ones who had normal jobs in town. Not artists, like his mother. He wanted to push away the fact that Mum was so different from them all, that her colourful clothes made her stick out like a parrot among wood pigeons. Her brightness was almost offensive here.

These strange, confused feelings choked Gyr. He wanted to throw a large, dark cloak over Mum and hide her. He wanted to quieten her strong laughter, make her be on time for things, make her be normal, and yet he knew he couldn't do that, and that he didn't really want her to stop being who she was. He loved his mother more than he could say. He loved the way they talked about things together, how they shared jokes that no one else knew or understood, how she always made time for him. Sometimes her being different from other mothers was cool. She let Gyr drive the car up the track through the Gate Field, and in the summer she was always taking him and Poppy off on unexpected camping trips and things. She was a great mother really, he just wished she didn't have to be so different.

Suddenly the drainpipe exploded with noise. A deafening roar shook the whole pipe and Gyr flung his hands up to block his ears. The sudden movement made him lose his balance and he toppled into the freezing water. He swore under his breath. The combination of shock and the intensity of the vast sound had left him shaken and he crawled limply towards the light at the end of drainpipe, completely confused.

'What was that?' Gyr said aloud. Not a car surely, he thought. What kind of lunatic would drive that fast on these roads? But now that he was out and into the secret ravine, he could no longer see the road and the car, or whatever it was, had disappeared.

With his ears still ringing, Gyr climbed down the steep waterfall and jumped onto the wide bank of the Lingaun at the bottom. Again, for perhaps the hundredth time since he had first found his special place, Gyr looked around in awe. The ravine was a wild spot, but not in that distressed way places get when people have been careless – there was no rubbish dumped, no rusting machinery. It was untamed, though not overgrown, for there was something here, a power, that seemed to look after the place. The old hazel and hawthorn trees that lined the steep banks of the stream were gnarled and twisted by the wind that swept down from the mountain, but they stood strong and healthy. Beneath them pheasant berry bushes stretched up towards the light. The ground itself, instead of being strewn with nettles and weeds, had a carpet of moss and tiny, white, bell-shaped flowers. It was these flowers, growing so peacefully and unexpectedly in January, which gave the place its magical and protected air.

Gyr headed down into the heart of his special place where the stream had cut a narrow gully that lent itself perfectly to dam building. He had spent much of the weekend designing and building a dam, now it really only needed one last and very important addition to make it perfect.

Gyr rooted about in the gully until he found what he was looking for: a large, flat stone. He took off his wet gloves and tossed them onto the bank. They were skiing gloves his aunt had sent him for Christmas. Back then he'd groaned about them being a useless present, but now he'd changed his mind. The gloves were just right for dam construction. With his bare hands he pulled away at the tufts of grass that clung to the flat stone and then, putting the gloves back on, he began to manoeuvre it towards his dam. The only way to move the stone was to lift it up onto one end and let it fall down by itself. Then lift again and let it fall. With each crash the stone sent up a spray of cold water, but Gyr ignored it and worked with determination. He had figured out that it was easier to look for stones upstream from his construction, that way he had the fall of the hill working with him when it came to moving them into place. It wasn't even that difficult to pull the stone into its rightful space in the dam wall, so that at last the dam did exactly what Gyr had wanted it to do all along, draining his man-made pool with a solid curtain of water.

For a while Gyr messed around, putting his boot into the sheet of running water and watching the patterns his foot made as it interrupted the flow. He found he could make a shape like a perfect arrowhead as the water shot diagonally away back into the stream. He stood there for ages, listening to the sound the water made and the way its music altered depending on where in the flow he stuck his boot.

Feeling very pleased with himself, Gyr sat down on the bank and watched the stream pour over the flat stone. It was mesmerising. He knew when Dad saw it he would say it was 'a shining example of good design and outstanding workmanship.' That's what he always said when he liked man-made things. Gyr wondered where his father was now. In his office, probably, designing some feat of engineering, or on a half-built bridge somewhere, telling people what to do.

Absentmindedly, Gyr picked up a stone. He held it in his

gloved hand. He wished Dad were there now. It had been so long since he had properly been there. Friends at school thought Gyr didn't even have a father. Gyr hated it when they asked. It was nearly the end of January and he had last seen his father at Christmas time, when he had managed to squeeze a week's holiday into his busy schedule. He was supposed to be there now, supposed to be living with them now. Back in August they had all moved over together. Mum, Poppy and Gyr had been there in time to start school in September, but Dad had had to go back to London to 'wind down the office' before he could join them properly and begin working from home. The winding-down operation was taking a long time.

Gyr held the stone in his hand, high above his head, and then he dashed it down into the pool of water behind his dam. A great wave sloshed over the flat stone, shattering the gentle rhythm of the flowing water.

September had come and gone, October, November, then December. Dad's arrival date kept moving forward.

Gyr picked up another stone and threw it. An explosion of ripples burst across the pool.

One week at Hallowe'en half-term, one at Christmas. Two crummy weeks. It wasn't much.

Without looking at what he was doing, Gyr's hand found another stone and lobbed it at his precious dam. This time he hit the wall itself. The impact of the stone dislodged a couple of rocks and water crashed over the edge, pouring out of the new hole.

Next time he phones, Gyr thought, I'll ask him straight out. I'll tell him I want to know when he's coming and no nonsense, no more 'winding down'.

The next stone Gyr threw forced a massive rock out from the dam wall, so the water behind it gushed out of his contained pool, down through the ravine. Gyr's large, flat stone was now left high and dry above the water level. His dam was in tatters. He thought of his father and how he would have loved the dam. A horrible, tight feeling stung Gyr in his chest, a pain that grabbed hold of his whole body and twisted it so that tears began to flow from his eyes. Blindly he charged into the middle of the stream, kicking out at the stones he had so carefully placed. He didn't care that his trousers were soaking up the icy water. He turned his precious flat stone over with his hands, feebly trying to toss it onto the bank. It slithered from its position and, yards short of the bank, sunk beneath the flowing stream water.

Then, not bothering to crawl back through the drainpipe, Gyr ran up the steep bank of the ravine, scrambled over the barbed wire, through the gorse and brambles of Old Mahoney's neglected fields, not caring if he came face to face with the old man. Not caring about anything except the terrible pain of his father's absence.

Chapter Two

GYRFALCON

These days Gyr thought about his name a lot. Being in a new school and a new place meant he had to keep introducing himself. Whenever he told anyone his name they'd automatically say, 'What?' 'Gyr,' he'd say, and usually he'd have to repeat himself. Then in an unwelcome echo of his little sister he'd add, 'It rhymes with fire, or higher.' If the person still looked blank, he'd grumble, 'It's from gyrfalcon, it's a bird of prey. It's like a hawk, but larger, and it has jagged wing feathers, like an eagle'.

After school one day, Gyr complained to his mother that he wanted to change his name, call himself John or James, something normal. Mum's face twisted into that pained expression she so often had nowadays.

'When I was pregnant with you, Gyr,' she said, 'the angels came and told me to call you Gyr. I didn't know what it meant, but when I meditated the image of a white bird flew in front of me. I looked it up in the library. You're a gyrfalcon. They're very rare white falcons from Arctic regions. Of course you can call yourself John or James, but I shall always think of you as Gyr.'

Gyr would always think of himself as Gyr, too, however much he winced at Mum's tale of angels. As he lay in bed at night he would stretch his arms out into the dark. Eyes closed, he would feel the gentle breeze stir at his fingertips. It would ruffle through wing feathers.

In his mind he could see the mountain behind the house and the valley stretching out below. He seemed high above everything. Suddenly Gyrfalcon would dive into the velvet air and fly away from Glenaskeogh. He would follow the tiny Lingaun as it grew from stream to river, thickening with white foaming water, coursing its way down the mountain, over the low hills, to the village on the horizon. There, Gyrfalcon would circle over the sleeping houses, he would skim the school roof and glide up to the top of the church spire, a white arrow piercing the dark blue night, a pale dart streaking over the tree tops. He would settle for a while on the roof of the house where Luke lived. Finally, Gyrfalcon would beat his mighty wings back along the Lingaun, back up the mountain, only stopping when he reached the secret ravine. There he would perch on the branch of a tree and look down on the tumbling water as it flowed past the tiny white flowers. White flowers, white water, white bird, shining in the moonlight.

Gyr didn't understand these sensations, and he didn't talk to anyone about them, but he felt the power of them deeply. Somewhere inside he understood that he was a bird and a boy, able to fly, but more often grounded. More and more during these strange days as he waited for his father to come home, there seemed less room in his life to be Gyrfalcon. He felt caged, trapped. Now whenever he thought of his father he felt a tightening pain. He felt everything in his body pull and push him, so that while it might appear to everyone else that he was still Gyr, the boy, inside he was Gyrfalcon, contained in a tight room, flapping between one wall and another, battering against closed windows in agony, desperate to escape to the clear mountain air, the soft sky and the freedom of flight.

Chapter Three

IN THE DARK

The phone rang, interrupting Poppy's tin whistle practice. Poppy frowned and took the whistle from her lips with an irritated pout, but Gyr felt secretly relieved – she was making an awful racket. He picked up the receiver.

'Hi Gyr. Are you coming dancing?' It was Luke's mother, Janet.

'I don't think so,' said Gyr. 'The car's in the garage. It needs new bushes. The mechanic's had to order them. It won't be back till tomorrow.'

'I'll give you a lift if you like. Ask Claire,' Janet said.

'Mum,' Gyr roared into the kitchen, 'it's Janet on the phone. She wants to know if we'd like a lift to dancing.'

Mum came into the room drying her hands on a tea-towel. 'I'll talk to her,' she said.

'Dancing, dancing, I want to go dancing,' Poppy sang at Mum's elbow, piping a few shrill notes into her whistle. 'Dancing, dancing, I want to go prancing. Can we go, Mum, please?'

Gyr rolled his eyes. '*Prancing*?' he said sarcastically.

Poppy stuck out her tongue at him.

Gyr waited to hear what his mother would say. He wanted to know too. There were Irish dancing classes every Wednesday night in the pub in the village. Gyr never danced, though some of the boys in his class did. It was Poppy who did the dancing, Gyr just ate sweets and hung around the pool table watching the older boys expertly shoot balls.

'Hi Janet, Gyr's right,' Mum said into the telephone, 'it needs new bushes. I don't know what they are. Ask Gyr, he knows about these things. Something to do with the engine. It's not too serious though. It just means we're stranded.'

Gyr stepped backwards, taking Poppy's tin whistle from her hands. It was light, like a baton. He twirled it in the air, watching how the metal caught the light.

'Give it back!' Poppy demanded.

'I was going to ask you if you could collect the kids tomorrow and bring them to school for me,' Mum was saying. 'I hadn't even thought about dancing, to be honest.'

'I want to go dancing!' Poppy wailed, trying to take the phone from Mum.

'Come on Claire, I can do that as well,' Janet said.

'Only if you're sure. I don't want to ask too much from you. If you're sure, we'd love it. Poppy really wants to go,' Mum said as Gyr tossed the tin whistle up into the air. He dropped it and the room echoed with metal crashing on the wooden floor. Mum sighed, 'And I could do with getting out as well,' she said.

At six o'clock Janet's three children swarmed into the yard. Gyr and Luke ran out to the haybarn to play on the swing. Soon Poppy and the others were there too and there was such chaos of screaming voices, excitement and people needing their turn that they were late leaving. They were made later still because Janet had such difficulty turning her long car around in the small yard. Gyr and Luke sniggered as the car went back and forth, inches at a time. Mum threw them a warning look.

'I'd better not drive this yoke in here again,' Janet laughed as they finally made their way out into the Gate Field. Luke and Gyr hopped out and carefully shut the two gates on the cows.

'Thanks so much, Janet,' said Mum. 'You've saved my life.'

'Well, I'd say I might have saved you a wetting at any rate,' said Janet, looking up at the large black clouds that were fast gathering. 'It looks like we're in for a bad night.'

Once inside the pub, Poppy ran off with the girls from her class. Gyr hung around his mother waiting for money for sweets.

'Here you are,' she said, handing him a few coins. 'I'd rather you and Luke played in here. I hate it when you go out the back and watch the lads play snooker.'

'It's pool, not snooker, there's a difference,' Gyr grunted.

'Whatever,' Mum sighed. 'They all swear too much.'

'They don't,' Gyr retorted.

'They do. You listen. Count how many times they say the f-word in one sentence. I tell you, if I catch you doing that there'll be no more dancing for you, that's for sure!'

'I don't dance anyway.'

'You know what I mean, Gyr,' Mum said, but Gyr had already walked away.

Later, Janet drove them back up the mountain. It was pitch dark and had started to rain, but when they got to the first gate into the field Mum said, 'We'll get out here, Janet. Don't want you getting stuck in the yard again. You'd never get out in the dark.'

'You're right. Out you get then. I'll be here in the morning, nine o'clock. It's very wet, Claire, are you sure you'll be all right?'

'We'll be fine,' Mum said, pulling Poppy and Gyr from the car. The doors slammed. Janet turned the car easily on the corner by Old Mahoney's. They stood in the rain watching the red tail lights disappear down the road.

'I'm cold,' Poppy whimpered.

'Me too,' Gyr coughed.

'I told you to bring your coats,' Mum said.

'No, you didn't,' Poppy said, so factually that Mum believed her.

'Maybe I didn't. I've said it so many times recently and you never listen. I guess I've given up. Perhaps this is a lesson for us all.'

They walked up the drive through the field, their feet slipping on the loose pebbles, the rain stinging their faces. The night was so black they couldn't see their feet on the gravel. From the inky field the cows' heavy breath sounded ominous and disturbing.

'We should have brought a torch,' Gyr said, angry that the night was so overwhelming. In London the constant street lamps had always painted the sky orange and you never had the unnerving experience of not being able to see a yard in front of your face. He didn't think he'd ever get used to the velvet blindness of a moonless country night.

It seemed to take ages to walk through the field, and by the time they reached the second gate Poppy was snivelling.

'My toes are shmeezing, freezing,' she whimpered.

At last they rounded the corner of the haybarn and came into the yard, stumbling towards the front door.

'Oh no!' Mum exclaimed.

Gyr and Poppy both jumped. 'What? What is it?'

'I've forgotten the key. I never thought about it when I left the house. Janet was kind of in charge of everything.'

Poppy began to cry.

'Come on, Poppy, there's nothing to weep about, the spare key is in the shed.'

'I'm getting wet,' Poppy sobbed.

'Next time we'll all wear coats, won't we?' Mum said grabbing Poppy by the hand and hauling her over to the shed. Gyr followed mutely. It was just as dark in the yard as it had been in the Gate Field, but inside the shed was even scarier, it was black as a mine deep in the earth. Mum crept in cautiously, using the wall as a guide.

'Where's the key?' Gyr asked.

'There's a little shelf on the back wall. Somewhere over here ... I think this is it ... Yes ... Yes ... I've found it ... oh no!'

'What, what is it?' Poppy squeaked.

'It's not here,' Mum said in exasperation.

'I thought you said you'd found it,' Gyr almost shouted.

'I found the shelf, but the key's not here. There was a biscuit tin, the key was in the tin. It probably fell down. I guess the cat knocked it.' Mum began to scrabble around on the floor. Something banged loudly outside in the yard.

'What was that?' Poppy cried.

'Just the wind,' Mum said, but her voice sounded scared. 'I've found the tin,' she went on, 'but I can't see anything else.'

Poppy began to cry again.

'We should never have let Janet drop us at the gate. She probably had a torch in the car,' Gyr said grumpily.

'I'm cold,' Poppy said.

'OK, OK Poppy, everything's OK. There's no need to be scared and there's no need to be cold. We'll find the key and be inside in just a moment.'

Gyr thought his mother's voice had never sounded so unconvincing.

She scrabbled around on the floor again. Gyr could hear her hands in the straw. He remembered weeks ago Mum had said rats lived in the shed.

'Ow,' Mum cried out.

'What is it?' Gyr breathed, hardly daring to ask.

'I scraped my hand on the wall. This is no good. We need a torch. Come on, we'll go down to Old Mahoney.'

Mum held Poppy's hand and led them out of the shed. Gyr stumbled and tripped on a box. The contents spilled out with a great clatter as if it were a drawer of cutlery.

'Hold my hand,' Mum said and Gyr reached out for it through the cloying darkness. When he finally found her warm fingers it was like a ship reaching harbour. He held on tight.

They walked back down through the field. The cows stirred restlessly, following them with what seemed like threatening intent.

'Nothing to be afraid of,' Mum said brightly, but Gyr knew she was terrified. He knew she was thinking what if Old Mahoney were out, what if he had no torch, what if they had to walk to Janet's house, four miles away down tiny, unlit lanes. They might meet anyone, or anything.

Poppy's whining had become one long note of sorrow.

'Come on, Poppy, cheer up. Think how many words rhyme with key,' Mum suggested.

'Key, me, can't see, want tea ... soaking wet, shouldn't be, get home, shall we?' she whispered, her voice dissolving into the rain.

They could see nothing in the field. Their feet found the gravel path more by the accident of stumbling off the grass and onto it rather than anything else. Gyr looked up and could just make out his mother's ghostly pale face. Far away on the smoky horizon he could see the tiny lights of the village. It looked cosy and sensible down there, it looked safe. Poppy's face was hidden from Gyr by their mother's body. She had stopped moaning and stopped rhyming, which meant she was too frightened to even speak.

Chapter Four

EMBERS

At last they made it to the bottom of the field. Gyr opened the last gate and shut it behind them. They could see a light coming from one of Old Mahoney's grimy windows. Mum let out a sigh of relief. 'Thank goodness, he's in.'

Poppy squeezed Mum's hand even more tightly. She was afraid of Old Mahoney on a clear sunny day, let alone on a rainy winter's evening.

They crossed the yard slowly, trying not to bump into the abandoned pieces of machinery and general clutter that lay around. Mum knocked on the door.

The rain started falling more heavily as they stood there, the yard filling with the sound of it battering on the tin roofs of Old Mahoney's sheds. Gyr listened to the rhythm the water made as it drummed heavily on the metal and burst from blocked drainpipes to ricochet off rusty oil drums, broken tin pots and empty gas canisters, creating a music of neglect.

They could hear a noise in the hallway, then suddenly the yard light went on, illuminating the whole sorry scene. Huge drops of rain were teeming down, rolling off Mum's wet hair, dripping from her nose. The door creaked open and Old Mahoney's rough, unshaven face glared out at them.

'Hello Mr Mahoney, it's only us, the people from next door,' Mum said, the words catching somewhere in her throat. 'I was wondering ... have you a torch we could borrow, please?'

'Bad night,' Old Mahoney said, and he turned around and shut the door.

Gyr and Poppy looked at their mother in disbelief.

Then the door reopened and he came out again holding a scruffy red torch.

'Could do with new batteries,' he grunted.

'Oh Mr Mahoney, you're a life-saver,' Mum gushed. 'Thank you so much. We'll bring it back tomorrow, I promise.'

Mr Mahoney nodded. He looked down at the wet, shivering children.

'Bad night,' he said again. 'You'd best get back to the fire.' He closed the door and they could hear him shuffling away behind it.

They left the reassuring light of Old Mahoney's yard and walked reluctantly back into the darkness of the field. Mum tried the torch, a dim glimmer, now stronger, now weaker, flickered as her hand shook.

'It'll do,' she said, more hopefully. 'We'd better not waste it going home though.'

They made their way through the blinding night, the rain now running in a small river down the path through the field. Finally they reached their yard. Back in the shed the torch spluttered and wavered as Mum rummaged in the straw.

'Here. Here. I've found the key,' she shouted triumphantly, leading them from the shed.

They practically ran across the dark yard to the front door.

'We'll soon dry off by the fire,' Mum said, turning the key in the lock and pushing the door in. They tramped into the kitchen, cold and wet, raindrops sliding off their clothes into puddles on the floor. In silence they stared at the fireplace. The fire in the grate was nothing more than ashes and a few red embers. Mum looked defeated.

'We could get it going again with some kindling,' Gyr suggested.

'Kindling's out in the shed,' Mum said wearily, putting the torch down on the kitchen table. 'And we'd only need more coal as well. I've done enough journeys in the dark for one night. It's late. We'll all go to bed.'

Gyr stared at his mother.

'Mum, it's five to ten. You never go to bed so early!'

'Well, tonight I'm going to. Anybody want to sleep in my bed with me?' she asked.

'Oh yes, can we, Mum, can we?' Poppy jumped up and down in delight.

'Come on,' Mum smiled weakly. She turned out the lights downstairs and ushered them up to her bedroom. They cleaned their teeth sitting up in bed, spitting into an empty mug. Mum borrowed Gyr's toothbrush. Then she climbed under the duvet, nestling in between her two children. She read them a story and long before the words 'The End', Poppy had fallen asleep.

'Good night, Gyr. Thanks for your help today,' Mum said, kissing him goodnight.

Gyr closed his eyes. He lay awake for what seemed like hours. Sleep evaded him. His mother felt warm beside him in the bed, he liked that. She lay beside him quietly, occasionally turning the pages of her book. Gyr pretended to be asleep. He wrapped his arms tight around his body. He didn't want to think about Gyrfalcon tonight, he wanted to stay close to Mum. He kept remembering her face out in the field, how frightened she had seemed. At last Mum turned out the light. Gyr settled down, he opened his eyes to the dark and closed them again. This time he thought he really might sleep, but then he heard a small sobbing noise, a kind of quiet choking close by. His mother was crying. Gyr reached out his hand and stroked her arm.

'Don't cry, Mum,' he said.

'I'm all right really,' Mum whispered through her sobs.

'Don't cry, Mum, don't cry. You were right, Seamus Maher said the f-word twenty-two times in one sentence. I counted, Mum.'

Mum snorted, in the dark Gyr knew she was laughing and crying.

Chapter Five

MOUNTAIN ASH

On Friday when Mum picked Gyr and Poppy up from school she had a black-and-white sheepdog pup in the car.

'The man at the dog pound said he'd never sit still on the floor for me, but he did, all the way home. He's gorgeous, isn't he?' Mum said, stroking the dog's head.

'But you hate dogs, Mum!' Gyr said, looking at her in disbelief.

'I don't like dogs very much, it's true. But I thought it was a good idea, living where we do. Everybody in the country has a dog.'

'Hup, hup, pup, pup,' Poppy said, leaning forward from the back seat to stroke him.

'He's not a pup,' Gyr growled, 'he's a dog.'

'The man at the pound said he wouldn't grow any more. I told him I wanted a small dog. He's about six months old already.'

'But Mum,' Gyr exploded, 'look at the size of his feet. Dad said you can tell the size a dog will grow to by its feet. That dog's going to be *huge*.'

'Well, the man at the pound said he wouldn't grow any more. Maybe Dad's wrong.'

'Maybe the man in the pound is wrong, Mum. He's going to be huge,' Gyr repeated, shaking his head at his mother.

'Look, huge or not he's going to be perfect,' Mum said impatiently.

In the back of the car Poppy began a quiet song, 'He's wrong and Dad's gone, Dad's wrong and he's gone.'

Gyr caught Mum glancing at Poppy's reflection in the rear-view mirror. For a moment, he thought she was going to cry. When she spoke again her voice was softer.

'You're right, Gyr, I don't like dogs much, but last night I prayed to the goddess Brigid for a perfect dog for our family. I said to her: if it's right that we should have a dog, then please have a good one at the pound tomorrow. The man at the pound said this dog was special, he has a very good nature. Well ... today is Brigid's day, and here's our dog.'

'She's not a goddess, she's a saint. It's *Saint* Brigid's Day, Mum,' Gyr grumbled, not in the mood to humour her.

'Gyr, is there a law that says you have to be negative all the time?' Mum asked quietly.

'Look, Mum,' Poppy said, pulling a battered drawing out of her schoolbag. 'We did pictures. Teacher said the bad king only allowed Brigid a piece of land the size of her cloak, so she put her cloak on the ground and it grew and grew until she had enough land to build a church.' Poppy laughed at the story. 'I like Brigid, Mum, she's kind.'

Mum relaxed a little, 'Yes, she is, whether she's a saint, or a goddess. She's sent us a perfect dog.'

'What's his name?' Gyr asked, scowling. 'What do the angels say his name is then?' he added sarcastically.

Mum couldn't help laughing at Gyr's bad temper.

'His name is Ash,' she said, smiling at the dog. 'That's Brigid's tree, you see. Well, I mean, the mountain ash is, the rowan. It's the sacred tree for February. Brigid's tree, Brigid's day, Brigid's dog. Ash.'

Gyr winced. He was going to be the only person for miles around whose dog was named after a sacred tree.

'Can we take him for a walk? Can we give him a bone, can we?' Poppy bounced up and down on the seat. 'I want to sit in the front and hold him.'

'No, Poppy, it might be a bit much, he's still only just getting used to us. We'll take him home and give him a bed of his own. Shall we, Ash? You're a good boy. You're going to grow up to be a great guard dog, aren't you?' Mum said, patting the dog on the head.

It was another two weeks before the Saturday when Dad rang to say that he was coming home – in late-February, for half-term.

'Is that it? Is the winding-down over? Are you coming home?' Gyr cheered into the telephone, pushing Poppy away with his free hand as she fought for the receiver.

'I want to talk to him too! That's not fair,' Poppy shouted.

'No, Gyr, no ...' Dad was saying, but his voice was lost in the noise of their squabbling.

'Be quiet, Poppy, would you?' Gyr shouted at her, but then he looked at her determined little face, sighed, relented and handed her the phone. She jabbered away to Dad for a while and then insisted on playing her tin whistle for him. Gyr fetched it and held the phone close to the instrument while Poppy squeaked her way through the rough bars of the piece she had been practising for days. He tried to smile encouragingly at her as she struggled to get the notes right, but he found his attention wandering from her to the telephone and his father.

At last, when Poppy had finished, he heard his father say, 'I have to come back to London again afterwards. I can only stay a few days.'

Gyr and Poppy exchanged a glance.

When Gyr finally put the phone down his feet felt like lead and he could barely walk from the room.

Mum stood at the sink, washing-up.

'That's nice, Dad's coming,' she said with a strange cheeriness he did not like.

'He's not staying though, is he?' Gyr challenged, as if it were all Mum's fault.

Gyr felt trapped, the kitchen window seemed to be waiting for Gyrfalcon's body to break against. He looked around desperately and saw Ash's lead hanging on the back of the kitchen door.

'I'm going to take Ash for a walk,' he said suddenly, hurrying his words as he tried to get out of the house quickly.

'Be careful, he doesn't always come when you call him. Don't let him off the lead. Really Gyr, I mean it,' Mum said, for she had seen the rebellious look in Gyr's eye. 'The mountain is covered in sheep at the moment, any day now they'll be having their lambs. Ash might worry them and if he does they'll lose their lambs. If he's seen chasing sheep, he'll be shot. They'd be right to do it, too. You can't have a wild dog in sheep country. So keep him on the lead,' Mum shouted hopelessly after Gyr.

Gyr went out the back gate and up the little boreen that led to the small reservoir behind their house and on up towards the higher slopes of the mountain. Ash pulled him, tied him in knots with the lead and generally made a nuisance of himself. Gyr didn't mind, he liked the dog and felt a certain pride in taking him for a walk.

When they came to the reservoir, Gyr sat for a while skimming stones, watching the ripples as they spread out across the water. In August, Dad had set a record of seven skips across the surface. Now Gyr tried to beat that, but he only managed a couple of graceless throws.

'That's nice, Dad's coming,' Mum had said. Why had she sounded so odd? Gyr wondered, lost in his thoughts. He remembered back in October when Dad had told them he was coming for Hallowe'en, Mum had danced with Poppy around the kitchen singing, 'I'm getting married in the morning, ding dong the bells are gonna chime'. A silly song if you were already married, but Mum always sang silly songs when she was happy.

Gyr tried to skim another stone, but it sank into the water after only two skips. Gyr sighed, a long deep thought escaping with the air that rushed up from his lungs. Something was wrong. He knew that. Mum, by the sink, with that smile, a funny smile, an awkward smile, a not-real smile. Dad still not coming to stay for good, and he was always so vague on the phone these days, never really saying anything. Something was definitely wrong.

Ash twisted and turned at the end of his lead.

'What's up, pup? Want to run?' Gyr said to the dog.

He looked around. The sheep were all much higher up the mountain, up towards Three Waters Meet where the earliest traces of the Lingaun came together in one channel. A wild spot up there, Gyr thought. A bit open, a bit too windswept. For a minute he wished he hadn't come this way and had taken Ash to the secret ravine instead. He looked down at the dog.

'OK boy, but just for a while, and mind you leave those sheep alone,' Gyr said, tousling Ash's head and unclipping the lead. Ash wagged his tail and ran to the reservoir edge, sniffing at everything. He bounded back to Gyr and then over to the pond again, running along the edge until he found somewhere to get a drink.

Gyr wondered what Dad would make of Ash, and Mum's insistence that the dog would grow no bigger. He smiled to himself. He remembered that Mum had promised they could have a bonfire to burn the Christmas tree when Dad next came, provided Gyr collected the wood. They'd be able to do that now. He had noticed there were a lot of sticks lying around under the trees that lined the boreen, so he set to work, occasionally throwing a stick to Ash to see if the dog would fetch it. Ash took no interest in sticks at all. He sniffed around in the undergrowth and ignored Gyr completely.

Gyr sorted the sticks into two piles, small and large, hiding them behind a clump of yellow-tipped gorse, its buds furled tight against the cold wind. He worked for a long time until hunger finally made him think about going home. It was only then that he realised Ash was gone.

'Damn!' Gyr said aloud. He looked everywhere. He ran back over to the reservoir, looked among the trees and undergrowth – there was no sign of the dog anywhere. Maybe Ash had gone home. He looked hopefully down the boreen, and it was then that the sound he had been hearing for the last five minutes finally recorded its proper message in his brain. What he had heard as persistent background noise to his activity was in reality the sound of sheep bleating. Distressed sheep.

Gyr looked up the mountain. High up there, somewhere below the gullies of Three Waters Meet, white bodies skittered and ran in all directions, bleating and screaming into the wind. In the middle of them, a wild black-and-white body danced and twirled. Ash!

'Oh no, oh no!' Gyr cried. He ran up the mountain towards the sheep. Images of dead lambs and injured ewes raced through his mind. He looked about wildly, expecting at any moment to see a farmer brandishing a shotgun. He ran as hard as he could, calling out Ash's name, but the dog ignored him and carried on blithely bounding between the terrified sheep, yelping and barking with the fun of it all.

The dog was too far away for Gyr, he would never get there in time. Soon enough, Ash would do something terrible and he would have a massacre on his hands. Gyr ran as fast as he could up the hill, his feet slipping on the stony ground, fear rising in him.

Gyr came to a place where the terrain was too rough for him to run anymore. He stopped, stood still, panting and wheezing, clutching at his side, which burned with a stitch.

'Come here, Ash! Ash!' he shouted, but the dog carried on with his rampage. Gyr watched in horror. Then, just as he thought things could not get any worse, he saw another dog, much bigger than Ash, moving purposefully down the mountain towards the sheep. Even from this far away, Gyr could see it was an enormous Irish wolfhound, as tall as himself. Whatever terrible havoc Ash might wreak on the sheep, this dog had the strength and ability to do something far more damaging.

Chapter Six

MOST DOGS ARE CALLED BRAN

The wolfhound raced down the mountain into the heart of the chaos. Bleating sheep fled in all directions. Gyr stumbled the last few hundred yards towards the scene, puffing, tripping and cursing. He thought his chest would explode with the exertion, never before had he run so fast, or so far uphill. He felt terrified of the huge dog, but he knew he had to do something.

Then, unexpectedly, the fearsome wolfhound sat down, still but bristling. It bayed three deep barks that echoed eerily over the moors, then stretched its legs out and lay waiting.

As if those barks had been a command, Ash suddenly stopped chasing his prey and flopped down onto his belly. The bewildered sheep still ran away from the dogs, but quickly sensing they were no longer being chased they slowed to an amble, regrouping into their flock. The odd bleat of complaint wafted down to Gyr's ears, but the sheep seemed none the worse for Ash's antics.

Gyr couldn't believe his eyes. The two dogs lay like carved

statues on the bare hillside. Nothing stirred except a gentle breeze. The sky was turning a strange sulphurous yellow, which Gyr knew foretold snow.

Gyr's breathing slowed and he began to calm down, to allow himself to think that everything was going to be all right. It didn't seem that anyone had seen what had happened. He would just go over to Ash, put him on the lead and take him home. He set off towards his dog, planning to give the massive wolfhound a wide berth, when suddenly he felt a hand land heavily on his shoulder. Gyr spun around with a gasp. The man who held him looked just as fierce, frightening and impressive as the wolfhound.

Gyr was caught. He looked up imploringly at the stranger who held him, but somehow words failed him, he couldn't think what to say, and the more he looked at the man, the more he couldn't think what to say. For Gyr had never seen anyone quite like him. He seemed so utterly out of place, so unlike the wrinkled, red-faced farmers who came to check their sheep in their uniform of wellies and tattered trousers with baling twine hanging from their pockets. This man was nothing like gruff Old Mahoney. He was strange, alluring, and although he looked out of place in one way, he looked to be a part of the place in another way, a part of the mountain itself, as if he had sprung up from the rock and heather, from the wild, tumbling stream.

Gyr stared at the stranger, taking in every detail, from his brown leather boots that had neither laces nor buckles but were tied with leather thongs to his suede trousers and plain woollen shirt. His long hair, which shone copper, gold and bronze, was tied back behind his head in a loose plait. His bronzed face was carved and angular, unyielding of any emotion, but the eyes, which held Gyr as fiercely as the grip on his shoulder, were a shining emerald green and they seemed to be full of laughter.

'Should have kept him on the lead, Gyr,' the man said in a low musical voice. He turned to call his dog and when he moved, Gyr noticed that at his waist the bronze handle of a knife flashed from its sheath. It was a small light thing, its handle delicately worked with a pattern of spirals. On his wrists the man wore heavy gold bracelets and these were carved with birds, their heads and tails twisting into one another.

'Bran,' he called, 'here boy.' The hound obediently ran to his side and sat waiting for his next command. 'Call Ash,' he ordered Gyr.

Gyr nodded dumbly, still staring at the stranger in disbelief.

'Ash,' he croaked, 'here boy.'

Ash copied Bran and came quietly to Gyr's side. Gyr stroked Ash's head, more to comfort himself than the dog.

'You'll be wondering who we are,' the man said, smiling. 'I'm Finn, and this is Bran.'

'Most dogs are called Bran,' Gyr managed to whisper.

'Know why?' Finn asked.

'Oh yes. Our class did a project on Finn MacCool. He had two dogs, Bran and the other one, I can't pronounce its name. Bran was Finn's aunt, magically turned into a dog.'

'That's the story they tell all right. But it's not true. I only have the one dog. I needed a good dog to hunt with. A dog to watch over me. I prayed to the goddess Brigid for a fine dog and she sent me Bran. Best dog I've ever seen. But you're not so bad either, are you Ash?'

Ash looked up at Finn, wagging his tail in delight.

'It's Cumhail, by the way.'

'Pardon,' said Gyr, confused.

'Mac-Coo-ill. Son of Cumhail. Not Cool.'

Gyr frowned. What was going on? Then it occurred to him that this must be some kind of joke of Mum's. It had to be. People hereabouts didn't dress like Finn, they didn't talk about getting their dog from the goddess Brigid, unless they were Mum, of course, they didn't know your name unless someone had told them first and they certainly didn't claim to be Finn MacCumhail. Mum. It all pointed to her.

Gyr's top lip curled in a questioning scowl and he was about to tell 'Finn MacCumhail' that the joke was over when something strange happened. The earth seemed to turn to water beneath him. It heaved like an ocean wave and his legs felt as if they were about to give way. He stretched out his hands, grasping for balance. In his chest he felt a sudden urgent stirring, felt feathered wings brush through him as if straining for release. It was as if the stranger's presence had called forth Gyrfalcon.

Nothing like this had ever happened to Gyr before. Gyrfalcon had always been his own deep, inexplicable secret. How was this stranger awakening the bird? Gyr's thoughts circled and then slowly began to settle. Months ago he'd been taught that if you placed a swinging pendulum in front of a still one, the motionless pendulum would begin to move too. His science teacher in London had called it sympathetic vibration. Something like that was happening to him now on the hillside, beneath the snow-laden clouds. The presence of this strange man was bringing some movement in Gyr to life. A new power ran in him, his heart beat slightly faster, his breath came more quickly, Gyr could almost feel the blood pulsing through his veins. For a moment he thought Gyrfalcon might burst out of his body into the sky, and it was this sensation that made him suddenly sure that this man was not ordinary. Gyr knew without a doubt that he really was *the* Finn MacCumhail and his dog really was *the* Bran.

Finn watched him, his face kind and wise.

'Come on, I want to show you something,' he said and started off towards the Lingaun with the two dogs obediently following behind.

Gyr hesitated, unsure what to do. Ash turned around, barked at Gyr and wagged his tail.

'All right boy,' Gyr said, 'I'm coming.'

Chapter Seven

UP THE LINGAUN

When he reached the steep bank of the Lingaun, Finn dropped down to the bottom of the gully where the water ran icy cold and roared with a voice swelled by recent rain. Finn hurried on up the mountain, following the path carved out by the stream. Gyr followed, trying hard to keep up with Finn and the two dogs. Finn jumped from rock to rock, or bank to bank, now on one side of the stream, now on the other. Bran and Ash followed his every move, never getting in the way, never needing to be called to heel. Gyr floundered along behind. He had torn his jumper on the brambles and his trousers were wet through. They clung to his legs and were cold, but Gyr didn't care – Finn had such an air of urgency about him that Gyr was only interested in keeping up.

They followed the stream until they came to Three Waters Meet. Here three small streams from different parts of the mountain converged in one channel. Today a great flurry of water rushed in their gullies, but Gyr could remember having been there in September when those three streams were dried up and the water ran only beneath the ground, faintly heard but unseen. Finn took the path of the central stream and headed straight on, upwards. They climbed steadily without pausing. The banks of the stream were now so high that Gyr wasn't sure whereabouts they were: somewhere up on the moors, further than he had ever walked with Mum and Poppy.

Finn stopped abruptly. He motioned to Bran and Ash to stay.

'We'll leave the dogs here. We'll be quieter without them,' he said, his voice almost a whisper.

On all fours, Finn scrambled up the side of the steep bank. Gyr tried to follow him, but slipped back down several times. Finn waited for him, but eventually slid down to give Gyr a hand up. He seemed to find Gyr's difficulty funny and kept grinning at him. Together they reached the top of the bank and Finn pulled himself over the top and lay still for a moment, face flat to the ground.

Gyr copied him. He was glad to stop, they had come a long way and he was tired. He lay there, his face on the ground, and then lifted his head, confused. They were lying in leaves. Brown and red autumn leaves covered the ground. Gyr looked about him. They were in a forest and huge trees reached up towards a blue sky. Pale sunlight broke through the sparse canopy of orange leaves high above their heads, casting a broken jigsaw of light and shadow onto the forest floor.

Gyr looked at Finn in a sort of panic. Finn seemed calm enough. Perhaps he didn't know what Gyr knew. There shouldn't be trees on the mountain, there hadn't been any for hundreds of years. High up, wherever it was they were, there should only be heather and rocks, a few hardy sheep, the odd bird. There certainly shouldn't be trees, and there couldn't possibly be autumn trees because it wasn't autumn, it was February, and half an hour ago when Gyr had looked at the sky it had been yellow and threatening to snow. Gyr was dumbfounded.

'Come on, we'd better hurry,' Finn said, getting up and leading a path through the trees. Obviously he knew where he was going, obviously he knew every leaf, tree and pathway of this unfamiliar landscape.

'Don't break the twigs so,' Gyr heard Finn say. 'Tread between them as I do.' It was as if he had whispered in Gyr's ear, but Finn was far ahead, darting in and out between the trees.

Gyr remembered reading about the Fianna in school. He had been fascinated by the stories of their training, when they learned to run through a forest without breaking a single twig. He looked about him, the forest floor was covered with twigs. How could he move without breaking one? Slowly, he lifted his leg and placed his foot in an empty space on the bare earth. He looked around for his next move. He looked ahead at Finn who was moving quickly and noiselessly through the trees. Gyr sighed in exasperation: how did the Fianna do this?

'Come on, Gyr, hurry, we'll be too late.' Again the voice in his ear like a whisper, again Finn much too far ahead for his voice to carry.

It was almost too much for Gyr. He was trying to hurry, he was trying not to break any twigs, he was trying to make sense of where he was and how it could possibly be autumn. How was Finn talking to Gyr, when he was so far ahead?

Where were they going? Gyr's head ached with all his unanswered questions.

The ground began to slope uphill again, they were climbing another bank. Finn dropped down onto his belly and crawled silently through the leaves like a cat stalking its prey. Gyr copied. The leaves stuck to his arms and legs, they blew up into his mouth and he spat them and their musty taste from his tongue. His heart thudded loudly in a rhythm of exertion and excitement. What had Finn brought him to see? Gyr had immediately trusted and followed him, but had he been right to do so? With his body full of the drama of his heartbeat, he couldn't cool his thoughts to decide.

'Not a sound,' said Finn's voice in Gyr's ear. 'They're just on the other side of this ridge.'

Chapter Eight

KING STAG

When they stuck their heads up over the ridge they were looking down onto a wide clearing. The ground dipped beneath them into an oval, shaped like a bowl, the edges of which curved up into steep banks on all sides so that the centre was a protected hollow. Around the hollow grew massive ancient beech trees, stretching upwards like solid stone pillars.

Gyr drew in his breath. He and Finn lay on the edge of a cathedral of beeches. Its roof was the arching lattice of branches overhead. Its sides were the red and yellow leaves, translucent as stained-glass windows with the sunlight behind them. In the centre of the clearing, their noise muffled by the layers of leaves, were two great stags engaged in fierce combat.

They were heroic beasts, large and muscular. Gyr's heart grew tight with excitement. He could clearly see the two animals. The larger one was obviously the elder, his greying coat was matted with mud but he held his head regally and his eyes were fearless and cold. King Stag. Gyr heard the words echo towards him. King Stag, leader of the herd, but now it was autumn and his antlers had fallen and his place was being challenged by a younger stag. Watching them fighting, Gyr felt a sort of rebellious disloyalty to the king. He had such an air of superiority, such a rigid, powerful authority that at once Gyr wanted him to lose the fight. His desire for the King Stag to be defeated was fuelled by the beauty and strength of the young stag, the contender. The younger beast was a prince in Gyr's eyes. He flashed through the cathedral like a red arrow of flame. His coat shone with health, his eyes burned with passion. On his head a fine pair of antlers towered above him nobly, like bone antennae tuned to the heavens above.

Gyr immediately loved the prince's sleek grace. He wanted to reach out and touch the animal, to feel the rippling muscles beneath its burning hide. More, he wanted to become the beast, to move into its body and help him fight. He wished that, like the heroes of old, he could magically shape-shift and transform himself into a stag. Here, on the edge of the cathedral of beeches, watching the two massive animals, he knew he would become the prince if he had the choice.

The prince stag charged at the King, threatening him with antlers that looked as sharp as knives. The King Stag reared on its back legs and pounded at the young buck with his hooves. It looked for all the world as if the young stag would win; the King was so exposed and vulnerable without his antlers. Gyr stared at the young animal's beautiful proud eyes and his only thoughts were of the creature's need to plunge his antlers into the soft breast of the King Stag.

King Stag reared once more on his back legs and bellowed, a huge, angry sound that tore through the cathedral, bouncing off the tall grey tree trunks. It was caught by the leaves in the orange canopy above and thrown back at them all, ringing out over the whole forest. With his bellow the King Stag charged the Prince, and with all the power he could muster he knocked the young stag to the ground with his mighty legs. He stood over the panting body of his young rival.

'Now,' Finn said in Gyr's ear, 'watch the young stag's eyes.'

Gyr did not need to be told, he was already watching, his heart weeping for the precious creature's defeat. The prince lay back, bristling with sorrow and anger, and then, as if a peace had suddenly descended upon him, his eyes filled with surrender. He lay still and the fight melted from his body.

The King Stag raised his noble head and pricked his ears to listen to the sounds of the forest. He stamped one foot on the ground, a warning of danger. Making sure that the young stag was following him, he leapt up the bank and bounded from the clearing.

Chapter Nine

WHERE IS YOUR SWORD?

Finn and Gyr walked away from the clearing and back towards the stream.

'Why?' Gyr asked. 'Why didn't he win? He looked stronger. He looked ... kinder. I wanted him to win.'

'Everything has its own time,' Finn said gently. 'Everything happens at the right time. If the gods and goddesses had willed it, he would have won. It was not yet his time.'

'But why not?' demanded Gyr.

'He is too young. He doesn't know enough. When the snows come this winter they will be fierce. Some years it happens, others not. The prince has never seen such snow. He wouldn't know how to lead the herd through it to safety.'

'Well, he'd try, wouldn't he?' Gyr protested.

'He doesn't know where the food grounds are to see them through such weather. The does would starve and die and in the spring there would be no new life in the clan. He would be King Stag of a dying herd. Is that what you want for him, Gyr?'

'No, of course not,' Gyr said, suddenly not so sure what he thought.

'His time will come. We must lose some battles in order to learn what we do not yet know.'

'Maybe,' Gyr said stubbornly.

Finn laughed. 'Must you always be right, Gyr?'

Gyr glared at him, but Finn was smiling in such an easy, open way that Gyr could not be cross for long.

They came back to the bank of the Lingaun and Finn called the dogs, who raced up the slope to greet them.

'Good Bran,' Finn said, stroking his head.

Gyr copied him, making a fuss of Ash, who had somehow put aside his puppyish behaviour and was now as serene as the great wolfhound.

Finn led the way along the top of the bank, above the stream's course. They walked slowly through the sun-flecked forest, always within hearing of the Lingaun. Gyr let its sound wash over him, he drank in the smell of the leaves and the trees. He found it so peaceful in the forest that he forgot to wonder about it all anymore. He thought of the stags and in his mind he could see them leaping through the forest, away from his scent. Gyr chased after the deer, diving through the trees, silently keeping pace with the beasts.

He was so wrapped up in his thoughts of the deer that he did not notice how the trees began to thin out and disappear. It was only when his feet crunched on something hard and a strange white light rose up before him that Gyr woke up to where he was.

'Snow,' he whispered, shocked. 'Finn, it's snowing!'

Gyr whirled around to look for the trees. He and Finn were back by the reservoir and the whole landscape was under a blanket of snow. He looked back up the hill, but the trees were gone, leaden snow clouds drifted over the mountain's peaks. The mountain had been transformed into a fairy-tale landscape, but there wasn't a tree in sight.

Panicking that Finn and Bran might also have disappeared, Gyr turned back towards the reservoir. There they stood, with Ash, waiting for him.

'What happened? How did it happen? Where did all the trees go?' Gyr demanded.

Finn smiled. 'Didn't you see? Where were you when we came down out of the trees?'

'I was with the deer. I was following the herd.'

Finn laughed. 'Gyr, do you know the story of the young warrior who wanted to be the very best and noblest of them all?'

Gyr shook his head.

'This warrior, he went to the High Priestess, asking her to teach him the Greatest Truth so that he would become a legend to be admired for all time. She turned to him and said, "Where is your sword?"'

Gyr frowned. He looked blankly at Finn. 'Where is your sword?' he echoed, not understanding.

'He doesn't know,' Finn continued. 'Maybe he left it at the door of the temple when he came in. Maybe he left it at home. He doesn't remember. The lesson is to be awake in every moment of waking. Where were you when the trees moved? With the deer.' Finn laughed again.

They walked on, down towards the gate at the end of the boreen.

'You'd better put Ash on his lead now,' Finn said to Gyr.

Gyr fumbled in his pocket. Empty. He checked the other one.

'It's gone. The sword. I mean, the lead. I don't know where I put it.'

Finn shook with soft laughter. He walked over to the fence where there were signs that a farmer had been feeding his animals. Bits of baling twine lay abandoned on the ground. Finn gathered up a few long pieces and plaited them together to make a lead.

'Here, take my knife and cut these ends, will you?' he said to Gyr.

Gyr hesitated, then he reached for Finn's knife, which nestled in the pouch at his waist. He drew it into his hand, a small, light knife, perfectly weighted. Gyr held the beautiful object in his palm, he closed his fingers around the handle and felt the cool metal. It gave him great peace to be holding Finn's knife.

'Cut the ends, Gyr,' Finn repeated quietly.

Gyr drew the knife to the twine and the threads cut like butter. He watched Finn tie the ends in a loop for a handle, then Finn nodded his head for Gyr to put the blade back in its sheath. Gyr tucked it into the soft leather pouch. Afterwards, he could still feel the coolness of the handle in his hand and as they began to walk homewards, Gyr felt the weighty absence of it being gone from him. He wanted to possess such a beautifully crafted knife.

They walked down the boreen in silence. Now that they were so close to home, Gyr thought of all the things that had happened that afternoon. He remembered the deer and the trees, the climb up the stream, meeting Finn, Ash attacking the sheep and how he'd not noticed because he'd been collecting sticks for a bonfire for when Dad came. He remembered Dad would be coming soon, and he felt sick and nervous at the idea. Finn watched these thoughts pass over Gyr's face.

They had reached the back gate and Gyr and Ash walked through it.

'Don't worry about your father's visit,' Finn said. 'The Earth is your Mother, She will look after you.'

Gyr turned around to glare at Finn in disbelief, but Finn and Bran were gone. There was nothing there except the dark evening drawing in fast over the snowy mountain, and in the silence the sweet, musical sound of Finn's laughter.

Chapter Ten

SNOW DAYS

That first snowy evening Gyr had come home wet and muddy, with bits of leaf and twig caught in his hair. His eyes had shone and before he could even sense that he might sound ridiculous, he had burst out the story of his afternoon. When he finally stopped his tale, Poppy had laughed, then got up and danced a jig around the table chanting, 'Gyr, Gyr, pants on fire. Gyr, Gyr pants on fire.'

Mum looked at Gyr. Somehow it didn't matter whether she believed him or not. He'd come home and told her Finn MacCumhail had prayed to the goddess Brigid for his dog. It was music to Mum's ears. From then on, as long as Gyr was with Ash, Mum said she wasn't going to worry over his whereabouts. Within reason.

Poppy was a different matter. She wouldn't let Gyr have five minutes peace without jumping out at him shouting, 'I'm the King Stag, fight me, fight me.' Gyr would have to wrestle with her, and then, antlerless, lose to Poppy's pounding hooves.

Whenever he was alone, Gyr found his thoughts returning

to Finn over and over. He felt as if he had been touched by a brightness, that something of Finn's spirit had come into his own body, so he was no longer dark and brooding. He resonated with the thrill and excitement of someone who has a secret, and his days were infused with an uplifting note that he could hear wherever he went.

At night, Gyrfalcon chose to fly up over the mountain instead of visiting the valley. Gliding high above the trees, he would search in the shadows for the deer and when he found the herd he would follow in the prince's wake as he walked behind King Stag.

And all the while Gyr pushed the fact that Dad would stay only a few days to the bottom of his thoughts. Maybe Dad would change his mind when he saw Gyr's special place, and Poppy and Mum, and how beautiful the mountain looked in its covering of snow. Maybe he'd stay.

Gyrfalcon swooped low through the cold night air, hope coursing through its body like its very lifeblood.

It snowed for several days. Mum didn't trust the roads so she kept Gyr and Poppy home from school. Gyr was in heaven. Now that he knew Dad was definitely coming to visit he had decided to rebuild his damaged dam, with improvements. His plan was to build a series of small pools that led one into another. The water would flow between the pools via a long, thin spout of water, or a short full blast, or a long full blast, depending on Gyr's fancy and what he was able to construct. Gyr spent the clear, white days in his special place. The snow lent it an even more magical air. The overhanging trees balanced a white ceiling above Gyr's head, giving him the impression that he was working in an ice cave. He lived in his Wellington boots and worked always in the skiing gloves his aunt had given him. Nightly, the gloves were left to dry in front of the fire and Mum and he laughed about how useful they had turned out to be. Since Gyr had met Finn, he and Mum laughed a lot more than they had for months.

The dam was coming along fine. Gyr now had all the foundation stones in place. He was working hard in the crisp morning sun when Ash gave a warning bark. Someone was coming. Gyr stood motionless, a massive stone in his hands. Down the side of the bank raced Bran, wagging his tail at the sight of them. Behind him, wading through the brambles, was Finn.

'Hi Finn,' Gyr called, sloshing towards him through the stream. 'Look at my dam, do you like it? It's not finished, of course, just wait till it's finished.'

Finn nodded and took a good long look at what Gyr had been doing.

'I was on my way home Gyr, I wondered if you'd like to come with me?'

'Oh yes!' Gyr said, dropping his rock, splashing water all over his trousers. 'Please.'

'Come on then, we'll walk through the fields,' Finn said, nodding his head to Bran who charged up the bank on the opposite side of the stream. Ash followed and gave chase, so the dogs streaked away over the snow, like arrows that Gyr and Finn had released from bows.

Finn led Gyr across six fields. Gyr counted. He was awake this time. He was going to watch and see what happened, exactly when it happened. They came towards Bradshaws's farm, but then veered right towards the mountain, crossing the mountain road and walking back along it towards a gate into another field. Finn swung himself up onto the gate. Gyr looked over it into the empty field. The snow had blown down from the mountain with the wind and settled in large drifts against the hedgerows. In the centre of the field was a circle of briars and scrubby hawthorn, marking the location of an old ring fort, which now was little more than earth banks and wind-knotted trees.

Gyr followed Finn up over the gate. He jumped down, and somehow, in the jumping, he found himself in another world.

The field was no longer white and snowy. It was no longer a field. It was a huge green grassy clearing cut from the forest itself, about the same size as the field had been. Gyr spun around. The gate had disappeared. Behind them a narrow path led off into the trees.

'Come on,' Finn called to Gyr and the dogs and he walked off into the centre of the clearing.

Gyr could only stare after him. There was so much to see. The whole scene looked like a fairground. There were coloured tents scattered everywhere across the grass. Some were low and round, others pointed like wigwams. There were fires wafting smoke into the vast blue sky, children running between the tents and animals shuffling and calling out their different cries. Gyr could see horses tethered at one side of the field, there was a wattle pen of sheep, another of goats, and loose dogs roamed contentedly between it all. Pennants and flags fluttered from tent poles and everywhere there were people, young men and women, gathered together, laughing and talking and greeting each other like old friends.

Gyr drank in the bright colours and the bustling scenes. He stumbled after Finn, but only managed a few paces before he realised he was hot. Very hot. It was sweltering. He looked at the trees that bordered the clearing: they were green, deep summer green. He could see the creamy-white blossoms of the elderflowers, hung on the green leaves like decorations. It was high summer.

He looked down at his hands in the famous skiing gloves. He looked at his three jumpers and laughed. He pulled off his gloves, ran his hand over his hot forehead and wriggled out of the jumpers without giving them another thought. Under his layers he was wearing a long-sleeved cotton vest, a bit white, but it would do fine. He kicked off his boots and his woolly socks and ran after Finn in his bare feet.

They walked towards the centre of the camp clearing. People began to notice them, they shouted greetings to Finn and waved to Gyr, his friend.

Finn guided Gyr and the dogs through the multicoloured tents towards a few low buildings that Gyr had not noticed before. They were fine, sturdy buildings, Gyr thought, casting his engineer's eye over them. Their stone walls ran up into thatched reed roofs. Gyr guessed that the largest building must be a hall or meeting place, for it was little more than a huge roof supported by stone-built pillars and heavy wooden beams. The beams had been carved with intricate lines and symbols similar to those on Finn's bracelets and knife. It was a beautiful building, yet too open and impractical to be a house.

It wasn't the buildings that so fascinated Gyr, however, it was the fine-looking men and women who wandered through the camp around him. 'Who are all these people?' Gyr asked, looking about at all the faces.

'They've gathered for the Standing Ceremony of the solstice,' Finn replied.

'But *who* are they?' Gyr persisted. They all looked so young and bright. The men, or boys, as they seemed to Gyr, looked so very healthy and alive, so strong and vital. They laughed openly, their faces full of adventure and excitement, so unlike the lads he knew who gathered around the pool table in the pub.

There were women here too, dressed the same as the men. Like them, they carried bows and arrows, or swords, or babies, or musical instruments, or a combination of all those things. Gyr stared and stared. There was so much going on. At one camp fire nearby a woman was telling a story, everybody listening attentively as she spoke, her arms and hands moving all the time as she talked, conjuring waves, or tree branches, or thundering horses' hooves in the air.

At another fire people were making music on odd-looking instruments. Others were singing, chanting in beautiful voices a song that went on and on, but the words never seemed to be the same.

'Who are all these people?' Gyr asked again.

'The Fianna, my bright warriors,' Finn said softly, staring at them with such a look of fondness that Gyr's heart twisted with jealousy and longing.

Chapter Eleven

THE FIANNA

A loud wailing sound trumpeted out across the clearing. Gyr listened, entranced. What he heard was a deep penetrating note that carried on the air, asking at once for attention. It was like a call from the earth itself, a long, low musical force that worked its way into Gyr's body, resonating against his breast bone. Finn saw Gyr's puzzled face.

'That's the horns,' he said, pointing to one side of the field where some of the Fianna were blowing into long, thin, bronze horns. 'It means the games are going to start. Come on.'

Finn and Gyr followed the throng of people who made their way towards the far end of the clearing. The games began with a furious horse race, where the entrants rode bareback on sleek, powerful horses. They galloped three times around the edge of the camp, accompanied by the cheers of the onlookers and the triumphant baying of the horns. Gyr envied the men and women who dug their legs into the horses' flanks and flew past, their faces shining with delight. A boy on a brown and white pony won the race. He took his winner's ribbon with such a look of happiness that Gyr's heart, which had felt heavy with dark jealousy, burst into the light of comradeship and admiration.

An archery tournament began over to one side of the clearing. The archers lined up in a row with their long, beautifully crafted black bows at the ready.

'They're made of yew,' Finn whispered. 'Very flexible. Watch.'

As he spoke the first archer pulled back his string and the arrow flew forth so fast its flight could not be seen.

Gyr and Finn stood amongst the crowd and every so often Gyr's attention wandered from the games to look again at the bright faces of the men and women of the Fianna around him.

'Why do they just get ribbons when they win?' Gyr wanted to know.

'These games are for sport, Gyr, for fun and entertainment. The Fianna are gathered here for the Standing Ceremony. There's no entertainment in that, it's a very serious occasion.'

'What is the Standing Ceremony?' Gyr asked, squinting up at Finn's intense expression.

'Once a year, in the heart of summer, we meet. I gather the Fianna from the four corners of the land. We feast, we sing and make music and tell stories of the time we've spent apart. We jest and hold these games. Then we become still. We meditate and fast and on the longest day of the year, in the twilight of the summer solstice night, before the sun wanes back into winter, we stand. We stand before the Spirits, and empty of everything but our Truth we bare our souls to the gods and goddesses and they judge us. They test us to see if we have stood for things we are called to stand for.'

Gyr fell silent. Questions darted through his head, galloping around and around like the horses that had circled in the race. What did Finn stand for? What did the Fianna stand for? How did the Spirits judge them? He wanted to know everything all at once. His lips moved with his unspoken thoughts.

'You'll see, Gyr. You'll see the Ceremony, though you're too young to take part. Another few years and you'll be able. For now you don't know the answers to the questions that the Spirits ask: Who are your people? What is your future? For what do you stand?'

Gyr flinched. Suddenly the sun felt very hot on his head, too hot. He shifted uncomfortably. Finn smiled at him and gently put his hand on Gyr's shoulder. Gyr felt the kind intent of Finn's touch. With Finn's hand on his small shoulder it didn't matter that he wasn't yet ready to stand with the Fianna before the Spirits. Gyr felt accepted as he was, raw and unripe, not yet ready to carry the responsibility that came with the Spirits' questions.

'Let's go in out of the heat,' Finn said, leading Gyr back towards the buildings. 'You're not supposed to know the answers now, you're too young. Think about them. By the time a warrior is eighteen he or she knows their answers. We stand every year to honour those answers and to ask the Spirits if we have upheld our calling.'

'What do you stand for, Finn?' asked Gyr. 'What do the Fianna stand for?'

Finn looked at him intently. 'Everybody stands for something different. We each answer the call of the Caller in different ways. Some stand for love, others justice. Some stand for the Earth Mother and some for the Dagda, the Spirit of the Universe. Some stand for their clan, or for the Fianna itself.'

'And would you ... would the Fianna ... kill for the things they stand for?'

They had reached the Great Hall in the centre of the camp and Finn was about to walk in through one of its wide openings. He stopped and turned to Gyr.

'We are warriors of peace, Gyr. We would not kill for the things we stand for. We would surrender our lives for them. There is a big difference. Know this, my mother was a High Priestess, my father was a warrior. I was their only child, but the Fianna are their sons and daughters. We are warriors of peace.'

'But you all carry weapons?' Gyr said as he followed Finn into the shadowy coolness of the great hall. For a minute, Gyr's eyes struggled to adapt to the change in the light as the low, dense thatch roof shaded the room.

Finn put his hand to the sheath at his waist, drawing out the knife that had so attracted Gyr on the first day they met.

'Look at this weapon, Gyr. Tell me, what do you see?'

Gyr was entranced once more, the reflective metal moved in front of his face and in it he saw the shadows of the great hall, the wooden beams, the thatch reeds, the carvings. Gyr saw sunlight bounce off its sharp edges and he caught fragmented flickerings of his face and Finn's as the blade almost danced before his eyes.

'I see your knife that cut a lead for Ash. I see all the things it can do, how it can carve wood, or shape leather ... and ...'

'What else? What else do you see, Gyr?' Finn asked quietly.

Gyr looked again at the knife, at the carefully wrought spirals that bound together the grace and balance of the handle and blade.

'I see beauty. It's bright and it shines ...' Gyr said, his hand moving up slowly as if he wanted to take the weapon from Finn. His fingers stretched forward and then suddenly curled and withdrew.

Finn nodded. 'You see power, Gyr. You see what the knife can do, don't you? It can create, or destroy.'

Gyr nodded his head very slightly. 'It can kill, can't it?' he whispered.

'The power you see in the knife does not belong to the knife,' said Finn. 'The blade only mirrors a warrior's own power. The shining brightness is within you.'

Gyr looked out into the field. He could see the Fianna moving over the green grass. The strong sun reflected off the metal of their swords and knives and glinted on the dark, polished surfaces of their arched bows.

'What you see are extensions of the warriors themselves, symbols of their own power, a vast power that comes into this world without allegiance. To serve the Caller we must choose wisely the forces to which we ally ourselves. That is why we Stand.'

Gyr hesitated, he looked at the knife once more and he felt a renewed longing to possess it. But somewhere in the depths of him he began to understand that the longing he felt was for the power of his own deepest essence.

'I only let my warriors carry a weapon when I know they value the true strength of what it is they carry. The Fianna are warriors for peace in this world, Gyr,' Finn repeated.

'But some of them don't carry weapons at all, they have musical instruments instead. Does that mean they don't understand their own power?' Gyr asked, at once feeling sorry for the musicians.

Finn smiled. 'The Fianna come armed in many ways Gyr,

never forget music and poetry can be as sharp as any blade.'

Gyr looked up into Finn's passionate green eyes. He sighed. He wished that he could be part of this, that he could join the Fianna and spend his life with Finn's warm presence nearby.

A chirping sound brought him back to the Great Hall and he looked up to see a swallow fly in from the gable-end behind them. It swooped in a long, steady flight through the great hall, over their heads and out the other end of the building, back up into the blazing sky.

'There Gyr, see that. That bird is like the soul. She flies from one great continent to another. She sees the marvels of the oceans and the lands beneath her wings. She lives for years and somewhere in those years she makes a small dive between two gable-ends of a building.'

Gyr followed Finn's thoughts and he saw the swallow in Africa and its yearly migration. He thought of the myriad things it must see on its journeys.

'The flight between the two gable-ends is our life on this earth, that is all we have here. But our soul flight is a much longer journey,' Finn said, looking straight into Gyr's bright, hopeful eyes. 'While you are here between the two gable-ends, how will you fly? Who will be your people? What will be your future? Which forces will you give your allegiance to? For what will you stand?'

'Gyr! Gyr!' An anguished cry from somewhere behind him made Gyr turn to see who was calling his name, and in the turning he saw the empty snow-bound field once again. He was standing in the centre of the abandoned ring fort, barefoot and in his vest, and over at the gate in the corner of the field stood Mum. She was holding his discarded clothes and staring at him almost fearfully, astounded by what she saw.

Gyr ran towards her through the snow, angry that he had been snatched from Finn on such a day, angry that their conversation had been cut short, but he couldn't help laughing at how the freezing snow burned his red toes.

'Everything happens at the right time,' Finn would have said, and perhaps there was some reason that Mum had plucked him back into the snowy field right at that moment.

'What in God's name are you doing, Gyr?'

'I was with Finn, Mum, that's where he lives,' he said, pointing over his shoulder at the remains of the ring fort. 'It was summer, really close to the solstice, and it was so hot. Wasn't it, Ash?' Gyr said as the dog raced up to join them. 'Ash'll tell you if you don't believe me. Ask him.'

Ash barked and wagged his tail and Mum's look of worry dissolved into a smile. She gave Gyr a quick, tight hug and handed him his clothes.

'I can see I'll have to have words with Finn MacCumhail if he's leading you a dance into the snow in your bare feet. Good thing I caught you when I did. Now dress quick will you, Gyr, I've got bad news. About an hour ago I found Mr Mahoney fallen over in his yard. I took him back to our house, but I think he's quite ill. I want to take him to the doctor.'

'To the doctor?' said Gyr, struggling into his second jumper. 'Do we have to?'

'Gyr, where's your kind heart? Mr Mahoney's ill and he's got no one to look after him. We're his neighbours.'

'Doesn't he have a grown-up daughter somewhere?' Gyr sniffed as they walked back along the road.

'I think there's a son somewhere in America or Australia.

We'll have to find him. Anyway, we're only taking Mr Mahoney to the doctor, I'm not giving him your bed.'

It turned out that they didn't just take Old Mahoney to the doctor. The doctor said he was very ill and very lucky that Mum had found him. She arranged for Mr Mahoney to be admitted to hospital immediately, and Mum volunteered to drive him there.

Poppy and Gyr spent a lot of the day in waiting rooms while Mum sorted things out for Old Mahoney and tried to get in touch with his missing son. For once, Gyr didn't mind all the waiting and hanging around, Finn's questions revolved slowly in his head, one after the other, all afternoon.

Who are your people? What is your future? For what do you stand?

Chapter Twelve

IT'S NOT TRUE

'Come on, Dad. Hurry up. This way. Sh! Don't make so much noise, Poppy will hear us. It's my secret remember. You're the first person I've told. This way,' Gyr said, leading his dad through the brambles in Old Mahoney's field. He waited impatiently for his father to make his way through the briars – he was so slow.

'Down here,' Gyr called, scrambling down the bank. At last his father caught up with him, panting and out of breath.

'This is it,' Gyr said opening his arms and showing off his secret at last. 'My special place.'

'Oh Gyr,' Dad whispered, slightly hoarse and out of breath. He stood on the bank taking in the magic of the place. 'It's brilliant.' He looked around at the mossy trees and gnarled branches. 'It's absolutely brilliant,' he said again, letting out a long, low whistle.

Gyr ran ahead through the middle of the stream to where he had built his series of dams and pools. All through the days of the melting snow he had spent every available moment building his dam. It had worked perfectly – the stream had lent itself to Gyr's engineering with such a will that even he was surprised. His first pool was small and deep, draining into the second pool by two thin spouts of water that shot out and away from the dam wall with tremendous pressure. They fell into the second pool, a medium-sized, medium-depth basin that Gyr had engineered to drain by his favourite method: a large, flat rock that forced the water to fall in a solid curtain. From there the stream tumbled into a final wide pool, which ended in a stepped wall that the water flowed over constantly, bubbling and singing to itself. The whole construction made a music that thrilled Gyr's senses.

'My dam, Dad,' Gyr said proudly.

'Oh Gyr,' Dad said. He stood back, looking at the dam, and he didn't say a word.

Gyr jigged from one foot to another. He had expected Dad to say what a shining example of good design and outstanding workmanship it was. He had expected Dad to be pleased, but not this, not this ashen grey face, this terrible look of tragedy in his eyes. His father staggered backwards, almost as if someone had hit him. He even brought his hands up in front of his face as if he were warding off blows.

'Oh Gyr,' he choked from behind his hands.

Gyr felt helpless.

'Dad! What's wrong? Don't you like it? I thought you'd like it. I thought it might make you hurry up and come home. I thought you'd see it and remember what fun we have and you'd come home ... soon.'

Dad made a strange, strangled noise that sounded like a wounded animal. Gyr felt a lump rise in his throat and stinging tears threaten behind his eyes.

'Come here, Gyr,' Dad sniffed, sitting down on the bank in

amongst the tiny white flowers.

'Here, sit on my coat. The ground's wet,' he said gently, rubbing away a tear.

Gyr sat down beside him. He said nothing. There was a long silence where nobody said anything at all. The stream ran relentlessly past them. Gyr looked into the water and bit his lip.

'It's a beautiful dam, Gyr. It's beautiful ... I ... I had no idea you could make anything so lovely, all by yourself. I was forgetting how grown-up you've become.'

Gyr looked up shyly at his father who was now staring into the stream, looking into it desperately as if the words he was looking for might suddenly float past and he could pluck them from the water.

'Gyr ... I have to tell you something ... I have to tell you, but it's very hard for me ... I don't know how to say it. I don't want you to ever think that I don't love you. I do. I love you and Poppy so deeply.'

'And Mum,' Gyr said, prompting, hoping Dad would say her name too. For suddenly everything that he had pushed to the back of his mind for the last few weeks came bursting up to the surface like a diver gasping for air. Gyr knew what his father was going to say. He knew it in his heart and in his bones. He knew it and he didn't want to know it. He wanted to yell out 'It's not true' before Dad said anything at all. But the words failed him. He sat beside his father, his mouth opening and shutting involuntarily, but no sound escaped his lips.

Dad turned to Gyr. He held his hands.

'Gyr, I love you and Poppy so much, but I can't come back and live with you anymore. I'm going to stay on in England.'

'No,' Gyr roared and the words erupted out of him with all the tremendous pressure of his waterspouts in the top dam. 'It's not true. You are coming back. You are. You are. Say you are.'

'I can't, Gyr. I can't,' Dad said, stroking Gyr's palms with his thumbs, unable to let go and wipe away the tears that rolled down his own face. He held on to Gyr's hands, knowing that if for one moment he let go his son would be gone from him like the stream water that ran so unstoppably down the mountain.

'Did Mum tell you not to come back? Was it Mum? Is she cross with you for taking so long to come home? Is that why?' Gyr sobbed, yet somehow knowing it was nothing to do with Mum at all, somehow knowing that she too was losing Dad.

'Gyr, you have to understand. I love Mum, I'll always love Mum, but sometimes life is very complicated. It's not like writing to Santa Claus and getting exactly what you want ... sometimes life sends us things we don't ask for. That's happened to us now ... to me ... I've met another woman ... and, you see, I love her too.'

Gyr shook his head. Life isn't complicated, he thought, life isn't complicated, life's very, very simple. Life doesn't send you things you don't ask for. He didn't understand the full meaning of what his father was saying, but he could guess. He'd had friends in England whose parents had found new partners. Gyr knew who 'another woman' was. He knew she was somebody who took dads and didn't give them back, didn't give them back whole like they used to be.

'You can come and visit me whenever you want ... in the holidays and things ... we'll still talk on the telephone ...' Dad was saying, but Gyr wasn't listening, he was trying to make sense of everything. He looked at his father sitting in the middle of the fairy flowers and he wished it were Poppy, and he wished that she did have on wings and a white dress and that Mum were there taking photographs and they were all laughing. He wished he'd never kept his special place a secret from them because if it had never been a secret then he'd never have brought Dad here, to sit in the middle of the white flowers and betray them all.

The ugly metal taste of betrayal filled Gyr's mouth, but he didn't know if it belonged to him or to his Dad. Somehow everything had become confused in his head. It was as if by keeping his special place a secret, he had somehow helped Dad keep his far more terrible secret, and now all these dangerous secrets were going to rise up together and hurt Mum and Poppy.

It was as if Dad had grabbed Gyrfalcon and fought him into a cage. As if Dad, his Dad, who said he loved him, who he loved more than he could explain, had thrust him behind bars and thrown away the key. Gyrfalcon screeched. He beat his wings against the cage. It rattled, but would not give way. He screeched again, flapping and fighting to be free.

Gyr tore his hands away from his father's. He ploughed through the stream and ran up the opposite bank. He ran and ran through the fields, away from his father who had struggled up the bank and was now calling out Gyr's name, uselessly, into the wind.

Chapter Thirteen

Gyr's only thought was Finn. He would go and find Finn. Finn would know what to do, he'd know what to say and he'd make everything all right.

Gyr ran through the fields and over the road towards the ring fort. But the field was empty. He climbed the gate, willing the same magic to happen again. He leaped over and landed in the field with a dull thud. Nothing happened. The scene stayed the same. Gyr ran towards the abandoned ring fort.

'Finn. Finn,' he shouted desperately.

There was nobody there.

Gyr turned to the mountain. He began to run towards it, through the field where the camp had been, past the ghosts of the tents and the horses that he so wanted to see. He ran, his heart and head pounding.

'Finn,' he called again and again.

He came to the boundary ditch and flung himself through it, scratching his hands on the holly and briars that tried to block his path. Then he was through it and up onto the mountain, his feet running over the heather. If he ran to the west he'd find the Lingaun again, but higher up than where Dad was. If he ran up the Lingaun maybe he'd come out in the forest, near the cathedral of beeches. Maybe Finn would be there somewhere in the trees.

Gyr made his way to the stream, keeping in low against the ditch in case Dad was looking for him. He wouldn't call Finn's name again until he was sure to be out of Dad's hearing. He didn't want his father to find him now; his only care was to find Finn. Finn would know, Finn would understand.

Gyr reached the stream. He dropped down the bank and ran into the scurrying water. He followed it back upstream, panting, struggling over the rocks, and pushing the undergrowth out of his way.

He scrambled up the slippery bank, saw the wild heathered moors of the mountain slopes and plunged back down to the water again. No trees.

On and on, higher up he went, further into the mountain's heart.

At last he came to the place where Finn had stopped the dogs that first day. He tore up the bank only to be met by the wild, empty mountain slopes once more. He staggered angrily into the determined, stubborn heather.

'Finn?' Gyr shouted desperately. 'Finn, where are you?' The wind took up his cry and wuthered it over the empty mountain. Gyr threw himself helplessly to the ground. He had wanted to see the trees, not this heather. He tore at the heather in his anger, but it fought against him, scratching his hands. A few withered blossoms fluttered to the ground.

'Heather!' Gyr sobbed. 'Damn heather!' He yanked at another bush, but it held firm against him.

'I hate you,' Gyr sobbed at the heather. 'I *hate* you,' he screamed.

The wind roared over him, took his words, snatched them up into the unyielding sky and threw them back, mercilessly whipping at him with their strength.

'I hate you,' the wind roared and the mountain took up the cry. Gyr's words lashed him. He didn't want to hate. He didn't want to hate the heather, or his father, or Finn for not being there, or his mother, or anyone, but his heart burst with its terrible pain. 'I hate you,' he choked, and the hatred came at him in waves of pain and abandon. He lay with the dead heather blossoms stuck in his fingernails, the wind blowing over him, as Gyrfalcon slumped lifelessly at the bottom of its cage.

Chapter Fourteen

CAGED

Gyrfalcon remained caged. There were no moonlit flights over the mountain, no circling of the village, no still moments in the secret ravine. At first it fought, desperate to be free, but soon it grew feeble, not even trying to lift its dejected wings. Days and nights had passed since Dad had gone back to England. Whenever anyone came close to offer titbits of food or love, the bird snapped at their hand. Gyrfalcon's life hung by a thin thread that might, at any moment, snap completely.

Mum tried to say all the right things, but there were no right things to say. Gyr was unreachable, locked into himself by his boiling emotions and the whirl of circumstance in which he was caught. Blinded by anger and betrayal, he could not see that Mum and Poppy were suffering too.

Sometimes at night, Mum would sit Poppy on her lap at the end of Gyr's bed. She tried to find things to say to comfort her children, but whatever she said seemed to isolate Gyr even further.

'The Connollys don't count,' Gyr snapped. 'Their Dad's

dead. That's different.'

'OK, not the Connollys then. Say we just count the kids in your classroom. There's twenty of them, right?' Mum was saying, she already had her hand up to count. 'There's you and Janet's kids, Luke, Ben and Anna.'

'Ben's not in our classroom,' Gyr muttered from his pillow.

'OK, so that's just three. There's Jack, he doesn't have a dad at all.'

'He must have one,' Poppy said quietly, looking up into Mum's sad eyes.

'Maybe the stork brought him,' Gyr said sarcastically.

'Of course he has a father somewhere,' said Mum patiently, 'we just don't know where. Then there's Peter and David, they live with their dad and their mum lives in Dublin. Sarah's parents live in the same house, but they're not together anymore. How many's that?'

'Eight,' said Poppy.

'Seven,' Gyr growled.

'Then there's that little boy of the O'Sheas who lives with his granny ... what's his name?'

'John O'Shea,' Poppy said.

'And there's Amy and Dan. That's ten. That's half, Gyr. *Half*. Now you tell me what's normal when half the people in your classroom live in not-normal families!'

Gyr scowled. He looked at the strange shadows the night-light cast on his ceiling. He looked over to where Poppy cuddled into Mum. He looked at his Mum's imploring face.

'We're not normal,' he said.

Mum laughed.

'I feel pretty normal. Look, Gyr, if I made you a mug of hot chocolate and you drank half of it, would the mug be half full or half empty?'

Gyr said nothing, the shadows on the ceiling danced in the flickering candlelight.

'Half full,' Poppy whispered.

Gyr rolled over and turned his face to the wall in despair. He stared at the blank paintwork and didn't answer his mother. It was obvious, wasn't it, that if you drank half your hot chocolate, your mug would be half empty. There was no question about it in his mind.

Chapter Fifteen

Bottle Digging

Gyr hadn't been back to the secret ravine since that horrible afternoon with Dad. He couldn't bear the idea. He felt Dad's ghost would still be there, reaching out for Gyr's hands as he sat amongst the white flowers.

At first, Gyr had felt bereft: he had nowhere to go. There was no sign of Finn, or Bran anywhere and after a while Gyr gave up looking. He stayed at home, baiting Poppy, calling her names, chanting Stroppy Poppy whenever she whined. He hung around his bedroom, bored and lonely.

He worried about Finn. Perhaps something had happened to him. That didn't make sense though, Finn MacCumhail had lived what, fifteen hundred years ago, maybe more, maybe less? He was surely dead by now at any rate. That was if he had ever lived. Maybe he had only ever been a legend. But if something or somebody was a legend that people believed in, could their belief be strong enough to make the legend actually become real?

These thoughts bothered Gyr like an itch he couldn't

reach, but what upset him most was knowing that the last time he'd seen him, Finn had said the Standing Ceremony was to take place in a few days. A couple of weeks had gone by since that day, so surely it had taken place by now. Even though Finn had said Gyr would see the Ceremony, Gyr must have missed it, for if that first day with Finn had been autumn, and the next time it had been summer, then time must gallop by in Finn's world. By now it could be winter, or spring, or anything. Gyr had no idea.

Added to that, Gyr was hurt and angry that Finn hadn't been there when he had needed him so badly. He tried to push thoughts of Finn to the back of his mind. He vowed if he did ever see him again, he wasn't even going to talk to him.

One afternoon, when Gyr had already wasted most of the day in his bedroom, Mum suggested that as Mr Mahoney was still in hospital, Gyr might like to keep an eye on his house and yard.

'You never know,' said Mum, 'somebody just might think of breaking in and stealing things while the old man is away.'

Gyr doubted he had anything worth stealing, but he dragged his feet down through the Gate Field anyway.

It turned out that Old Mahoney's yard was a great place to explore, full of interesting bits and pieces. The sheds were crowded and messy, crammed with old broken pots and pans, rope and string, empty paint pots, biscuit tins full of old tools and all manner of fascinating objects that no one had touched for years.

Around behind the house Gyr found the place where Old Mahoney piled his rubbish. There were a lot of old cans and empty whiskey bottles. They weren't interesting to Gyr, but he hunted about for a while like a rat in the county dump. The rubbish heap backed onto the ditch, a massive, overgrown box hedge that once would have been clipped and tidy. Gyr climbed over the heap and into the ditch, amazed to see bottles sticking up here and there amongst the roots of the hedge.

He pulled one out, a brown one. It looked old, much older than the fresh stuff at the other end of the heap. It had no lid and no grooves for a screw cap. He dug around some more. There were a lot of broken bottles in there, but also some that were still whole, some real beauties. They were all different colours – blue, brown, green, some clear – but the glass in them was thick and heavy, nothing like the bottles you saw nowadays. People just didn't make bottles like these anymore. Gyr poked around among the bottles for an hour or so. As he found them, he took the very best bottles out and lined them up in a row on the ground.

Digging around in the roots of the hedge, Gyr found a tiny bottle, no bigger than his hand. It had a little cork still wedged firmly in the bottleneck. Gyr rubbed away the damp soil that clung to its sides and uncovered a single word: Poison. Gyr turned it from side to side and realised the bottle was half full. His eyes widened and he breathed out slowly. Real poison. Why did Old Mahoney have that? What had he used it for? Gyr held the bottle and looked around. He wasn't sure if he should just put it back in the heap. It might be dangerous to take it home. Say Poppy found it, what then? Then again, Poppy might just as easily find the bottle here at Mahoney's, he reasoned.

For a minute, Gyr didn't know what to do. The bottle in his

hand bewitched him. He stared at the clear, harmless-looking liquid and he saw the destructive power it held. His hand shook slightly as he put the bottle in his shirt pocket.

Gyr looked over the row of coloured bottles he had found. He didn't think that the old man would mind if he took them, they had been dumped after all. There were, however, too many for him to carry. He'd have to go back home and get a box to collect them. But he could take a few with him now.

He loaded himself up with an armful of bottles and skirted around to the front of the house, made his way through the oily yard and was just about to come out of the gate when he heard the sound of horses' hooves clattering at speed along the road. He ducked in behind the hedge and waited for the rider to go by.

The pounding hooves came to an abrupt halt on the other side of the hedge. Gyr felt caught, then, to his surprise, a hearty laugh broke out and a familiar voice said, 'Are you hiding from me, Gyr?'

Finn.

Gyr put down the bottles he was carrying and stepped out from behind the hedge to see Finn sitting tall on a gleaming black mare. Gyr blinked at the shining apparition before him, impressed by the array of new leatherwork and gleaming brass that stood out from the black satin of the horse's coat. Finn, too, was dressed ceremoniously. His light white shirt was embroidered with small symbolic images picked out in golden thread. On his wrists Finn wore heavy gold bracelets and at his neck, like a bright half moon in the sky, was a gold torc, so polished that it reflected Finn's face, the hedgerows, the mountain and the huge sky above their heads.

'Are you ready, Gyr?' Finn asked smiling, bending down and extending a hand that would pull Gyr up beside him.

Ready? For what? Gyr didn't know. He looked up at the regal horse. He looked at the spirals and knots carved into the metal that Finn and the horse both wore. He stared into Finn's gentle face and dancing emerald eyes, trying hard to remember his vow never to speak to Finn again. Then his heart took a massive, daring leap and he reached up for Finn's strong grasp.

'Yes,' he said as Finn drew him up to sit behind him on the horse. 'Yes. I'm ready,' he whispered as Finn urged his knees into the horse's flanks and they took off up the tiny boreen beside Old Mahoney's house, cantering on, up the mountain, towards the wild heather moors.

Chapter Sixteen

THE CATHEDRAL BY NIGHT

They rode up the mountain into the dusk. It was not the abrupt dusk of a winter's evening, but the slow lingering surrender into night that only comes with summer. Gyr held tight to Finn's broad back, his face pressed in between his friend's powerful shoulders. He could see nothing ahead, but only look left or right across the grey-blue slopes of the mountain that rolled away like a quiet sea in the fading light. Suddenly, as if he were in two places at once, Gyr could see the ghostly forms of trees shimmering out of the gloom. He could see both the barren moors and the thick forest existing simultaneously. And now, as if they were truly in the trees, the horse's path curved and banked, speeding almost of its own accord into the twilight ahead of them.

Gyr folded into Finn's back as they leaned forward to avoid the low branches. Instantly, he became aware of the small poison bottle tucked in his pocket. It dug into his chest and he realised it must also feel uncomfortable for Finn. Gyr could feel his heart pressed tight up against the bottle and he knew Finn's heartbeat was there too, just in front of his own, separated from his by the small glass barrier.

Now a new sound came to him, a music that swelled and grew in volume so that Gyr realised they were travelling towards it. It was the primal din of celebration, whirling faster and faster as the horse sped towards its source. Gyr heard the bronze horns at the core of the wild mêlée. Drums, bells and crotals added to the medley, all following the lead of the triumphant horns. Over and above it were human voices, chanting strange, unfamiliar words into the warm night.

At last the horse's pace slackened and she eased to a canter, then a trot and gradually to a gentle walk. When she came to a halt, Finn jumped to the ground. Gyr knew the place they had come to. In front of them was the bank they had crawled up on their stomachs that first day in the woods when they had spied on the stags. A flickering orange glow lit up the beech trees that towered over the bank.

The music and chanting moved faster and faster as Finn tethered the horse. Together Gyr and Finn climbed the steep bank and stood looking down once more onto the cathedral of beeches. Flaming torches guttered and wavered with the music, lighting the cathedral, and in the golden, shadowy space beneath sat the men and women of the Fianna, tall, handsome and sure.

They were seated around a massive five-pointed star, woven from hazel like a wattle fence. On its arms, Gyr could see, were placed different objects: rocks and crystals on one, feathers on another, a small bowl of water on the next and a flaming rushlight on the fourth arm, only the fifth arm – the uppermost point of the star – remained empty. In the very centre of the star a large bronze bowl had been placed, a wide shallow vessel filled with water, on the surface of which danced mirrored ripples of the golden torches.

Finn bent towards Gyr and whispered, 'The different arms of the altar represent the elements – Spirit, Earth, Air, Water, Fire. The Spirit guides will sit at the altar and the Fianna will go forward to speak with them. Come, follow me.'

As they walked down into the clearing, Gyr looked about him at the glowing faces of the people he passed. Most of them took no notice of their late arrival, so busy were they in their music-making and chanting. The sound around them was so thick and intense it was like walking through water. Finn moved to the front of the crowd and sat down, just yards away from the hazel altar, close to the arm of Earth. He motioned Gyr to sit by him, right in front of the element of Air.

The wild trumpeting and drumming around them reached an ecstatic climax and then stopped suddenly. Not a note out of place, not a chime, everyone halted in the same instant and a deep silence filled the clearing. It rose up above the heads of the Fianna, reaching to the branches of the overhanging trees, which rippled and moved and, in so doing, allowed a passageway for the full moon to enter the clearing. The silver disc of moon shone down to see its face perfectly reflected in the bronze bowl at the centre of the altar.

No one moved. The warriors closed their eyes and their breathing became slow and regular. Gyr looked sideways at Finn and found that he too had shut his eyes. Gyr was reminded of the times he'd tried meditating with Mum, she got that same look about her. It always made Gyr want to giggle. He always had giggled, which had made Mum cross and she had given up trying to interest Gyr in meditation. The silence now was too serious, too impressive for Gyr to break out into giggles, but still he felt awkward. He tried shutting his eyes, but it didn't feel right. He wanted to watch what was going on. At last a sort of peace descended on Gyr, as if a liquid had poured from Finn's body into his own, so that he was able to be still and quieten the thoughts that raced through his mind.

A movement from the edge of the clearing caught Gyr's eye. Three cloaked figures were moving towards the star, their faces concealed behind shining masks of gold. Gyr could see nothing through the thin eye-holes of their masks, nor through the narrow slits that served for mouths. He watched the slow, stately progress of the Spirit guides as they moved to the altar, bowed their heads reverently and sat down. The Spirit of the Ancestors sat just in front of Gyr, with its back to the star's arms of Earth and Air. The Spirit of the Future moved to the place where the arms of Fire and Water met. The last figure, the Standing Spirit, more noble and forbidding than all the rest, moved to sit at the head of the star.

Nobody else moved. Nobody opened their eyes. Even the flames in the torches seemed to cease their flickering. Gyr felt awkward and slightly afraid, he was the only person there with his eyes open and he seemed to be the only person who thought the silence had already gone on far too long. He could see his face reflected in the golden mask of the Spirit of the Ancestors in front of him. It wasn't at all like looking in a mirror, the reflection moved and melted, distorting his image into something strange and almost ugly.

Gyr understood what Finn had meant that day at the camp when he had said there was no entertainment in the Standing Ceremony, that it was a very serious affair.

Somewhere behind him a slow drumming started and a lone female voice began a haunting song that eased itself into the silence like smoke joining mist. Around him the Fianna slowly began to open their eyes. Finn stood up and walked forward. He bowed before the Spirit of the Ancestors and sat down cross-legged in front of the masked figure. At this signal, a man and a woman in the crowd stood up and came forward to sit in front of the other two golden faces.

They began talking to the Spirit guides, their own faces solemn as they spoke and listened. Minutes passed and then those Fianna who had spoken with a Spirit guide went back amongst the crowd. Others moved forward to take their places and in this way the Standing Ceremony continued. The Fianna would go up, talk with a masked figure, then go back and contemplate what had been said. When they were ready, they would go to speak with a different guide until they had sat with all three.

The warriors wove their way through the clearing in a strange, slow ballet. Gyr watched this dance, he watched the faces of the Fianna as they sat before the golden masks. He saw different expressions of hope and joy, serenity, confusion and fear. Sometimes, especially with the younger people, Gyr would see faces moved with pain and sorrow and those beautiful warriors would weep. Teardrops would roll down their faces in the torchlight. No one took any notice, and even those who wept allowed their tears to flow freely, without shame.

Gyr had never seen anything like this before. He felt a great tenderness towards Finn for allowing him to be there, yet beside his gratitude a new feeling rose, mounting strong in his body. It was not enough just to sit there and watch the proceedings, he needed to belong, to be part of it. He desperately wanted to go before the masked figures and speak with the Spirits and be considered a warrior, like the others.

At last Finn, having visited all three masked figures, came and sat down beside Gyr once more. He looked at him with appraising eyes that seemed to see the creature of Gyr's longing. He said nothing. He gave no judgement as to whether or not Gyr should go forward. They both knew that on that day back at the Fianna camp, Finn had told Gyr he was too young to take part in the ceremony. Then why has he brought me at all? Gyr wondered. Surely now if he can read my thoughts he will repeat those words again, or say something else to hold me back?

Finally, Finn turned to him.

'They don't tell fortunes Gyr, they are the Truth-tellers,' he whispered, looking at the golden mask in front of them both. 'They look straight into our hearts. We don't always like, or understand, what it is they see there.'

Chapter Seventeen

THE STANDING CEREMONY

Gyr sat at the edge of the circle trying to quell his urge to speak with the Spirits. His desire had become a live creature, desperate to escape from his chest. He could feel it now, Gyrfalcon, beating its powerful wings, squawking and cawing from its cage. The bird struggled, fought, and suddenly the bars of the cage broke under Gyrfalcon's attack and he soared up into the air above the altar. The bird circled beneath the green canopy of leaves, drinking in draughts of freedom, its wings thrilling to the tiny currents that caressed them.

He hovered above the Fianna, looking down on them, on the star of the altar and onto the bronze bowl that now reflected both the white moon and the white bird. Gyrfalcon looked down at Finn MacCumhail and Finn raised his head to the bird. He gave a small, slight nod, and in that moment Gyr woke up and realised that the place in front of him was empty. The Spirit of the Ancestors behind the golden mask was staring straight at him. The next second Gyr was up and lunging forward to sit before the awesome mask. Nervously, he looked into the black holes where he knew two eyes must be.

'Who are your people?' A strange voice, neither male nor female, emanated from the Spirit. Gyr did not answer. The mask looked at him. Gyr could hear its breathing, somehow amplified.

'Who are your people?' It asked again and somewhere behind him Gyr heard the steady monotonous beat of a drum.

'City people,' he blurted out. 'Not warriors, business people. My father's an engineer, like his father was, and my mother's an artist, and her mother was a housewife, but her father owned a shop ... a big shop ...,' Gyr trailed off. He thought he sounded a bit silly and he felt very embarrassed that his people were engineers and shop-owners and not warriors.

'Who are your people?' the voice intoned again as if he hadn't spoken at all.

'City people,' Gyr tried once again, but the drumming pounded against the sides of his head and he couldn't think clearly. 'You know, they all wear suits and work in offices, except Mum, she's an artist, like I said,' Gyr fell silent, he didn't know what else to say.

'Who are your people?' the strange metallic voice said again.

Gyr felt very uncomfortable. This wasn't what he had expected at all. He'd said everything, hadn't he? His mind replayed his words over and over in a rhythm as relentless as the drumming. He felt completely helpless. He grew hot and his palms sweaty. Hadn't the Spirit heard what he had said? Had something gone wrong? Gyr looked imploringly into the empty eye slits, he could see something shiny dart inside the black.

'Enough now,' the voice said and Gyr backed away, nodding, relieved and confused. He returned to his place at Finn's side.

Finn said nothing, he did not even acknowledge what had happened. Gyr felt clumsy and awkward. He didn't know if Finn was angry with him, he couldn't tell. He could still hear the voice of the Spirit guide ringing like a bell tolling bad news: *Who are your people? Who are your people?* Above him, Gyrfalcon circled the clearing in a wavering unsteady path, as if even the beech trees were too confining. Someone blew a long, sorrowful note on one of the horns.

The noise roused Gyr from his thoughts. He looked up to see a familiar figure walking away from the Spirit of the Future. He recognised the boy who had won the horse race that day at the Fianna camp. Again the boy seemed to be glowing with some sort of inner happiness. It irked Gyr. Now that he thought about it, the horse-boy didn't seem to be that much older than himself. Surely he wasn't eighteen yet? He didn't look it. Gyr watched him sit down and saw the exchange of smiles between the horse-boy and the Fianna warrior beside him. Gyr burned with a longing for their comradeship.

The space in front of the Spirit of the Future remained empty. Gyr looked sideways at Finn, but he had closed his eyes again and Gyr couldn't get his attention. Gyr watched the horse-boy as he settled back amongst his friends, and before he could even understand the jealousy that motivated him, Gyr had leapt to his feet and was heading for the empty space in front of the Spirit of the Future.

'What is your future?' the voice oozed through the mouth of the mask, and Gyr shifted in his seat. Somehow it didn't seem fair to talk to someone you couldn't see. Gyr's face was open to be read and understood, but the eyes and expressions of the figure behind the mask were closed and unavailable.

'Well, um ...' Gyr faltered, the music behind him growing louder and more intrusive.

'What is your future?' the Spirit asked again and Gyr was suddenly filled with a dread that this would be a repeat of his time with the Spirit of the Ancestors.

'Um ... well ... happiness,' Gyr said. 'Looking after the earth ... the environment ... and ... love. There's lots of love in my future,' he said, becoming more sure of himself. Yes, he thought, that sounded quite good. Mum would be proud of him, talking about the environment and love. She always said that love was the only real reason that people were on the planet at all.

The Spirit of the Future stared at Gyr. It said nothing for a long time. Gyr could see his own eager face reflected in the golden mask. Now he looked gold and handsome, rather like Finn. The Spirit of the Future still said nothing and Gyr began to fidget. He dreaded it would ask the question again. Above him a cloud obscured the moon and Gyrfalcon flew up out of the clearing, away over the leafy branches of the beech trees.

'I do not see love,' the cold voice said suddenly. 'I see judgement. You always see the dark, you always look for the black, the negative. There is no room for love in your heart. It is closed with judgement.'

What? Gyr thought. Was the Spirit talking to him? Had it got the right person? Surely this was a real mistake now? Gyr was full of love. He loved Mum and Finn, and Dad, he thought sadly. He loved Poppy, even though she was annoying. His heart was full of love, he felt sure of it.

'Open the doors of your heart, let your judgement be blown to the corners of the earth, make room for compassion and forgiveness.' The Spirit of the Future nodded, 'Go now.'

Gyr stumbled back to his place beside Finn. He felt numb. He sat down and as he did so tears welled up in his eyes and began to pour down his face.

'There is no room for love in your heart. It is closed with judgement.'

Gyr wept. He felt he had been branded and condemned. He rebelled against all he had heard. It was the Spirit of the Future that was full of judgement, not him. He'd been so full of love for Finn and the Fianna, but not now, now he stung, now he was hurt and angry and ashamed. Raging tears of embarrassment and disappointment poured down his face. He didn't want Finn to see, he didn't want the Fianna to see. He stood up and turned around, weaving a stumbling path through the ranks of warriors. He reached the shadows at the back of the clearing, ran up the bank and into the dark embrace of the forest. From somewhere behind him, over and above the untamed music, Gyr could hear the high-pitched shriek of a distressed bird.

Chapter Eighteen

IN THE DARK

Gyr ran as fast as he could, tears streaming down his face. His only desire was to get away, as far and as fast as possible. He didn't think about where he might be going, he just kept running.

Soon the light and sounds from the Standing Ceremony faded and he found himself deep in the dense forest. The full moon silhouetted the trees with a strange white glow. It filled the forest with shadows and illusions. Several times as he ran, Gyr dodged trees that were not actually there or found himself snared in overhanging branches that he had not seen.

Once or twice he looked up at the blue-black sky overhead where small silver clouds hurried across the moon's surface. He hurried too, trying to distance himself from the boy the Spirit of the Future had branded, but however fast he ran he could not escape the Spirit's words, nor the burning pain they caused him.

Gyr ran until his body ached and his legs gave way beneath him. At last he hurled himself down on the forest floor. Around him the moon and the trees cast a dramatic display of light and shadow. Gyr lay without moving. The ground felt hard. His heart stung. He felt alone and rejected: he wasn't good enough for the Fianna, he had failed all their tests. He couldn't walk in the forest without breaking twigs and he couldn't answer the Spirits' questions. Worst of all, he had a dark heart, didn't he, whereas the others had all seemed so bright and glowing. He remembered images from the Standing Ceremony of warriors who had cried, as if they too hadn't liked what they'd heard, but he brushed those pictures away as if they were cobwebs. He was the only one who had run away from the Spirits; everyone else had stayed.

What hurt Gyr most was that he suspected the Spirit of the Future was right. It had looked deep into him and had seen judgement. Mum often called him negative too. Gyr wondered if his judgemental nature was obvious to everybody. Did Finn see it? Did his Dad? Maybe that was part of the reason he had left them all. A new wave of despair washed over Gyr as he thought of Dad. He hugged his knees into his chest and curled himself into a tight, angry ball. The small bottle in his shirt pocket jarred uncomfortably against his chest. It made him uncurl and sit up.

Gyr took the bottle out of his pocket. The glass glinted and gleamed in the moonlight and though his fingers shook slightly, he could still read the warning letters on the bottle: Poison. His heart raced and his fingers gripped the bottle tightly. He bent and sniffed at the cork. It had a bitter, almost almond scent. Out of curiosity, he loosened the cork a little. Suddenly the air about him filled with the movement of wings and a harsh cry tore him away from what he was doing.

Gyrfalcon swooped above him, skimming close to his head, then darting away before returning to fly over him again. Gyr watched, stunned. The bird moved through the trees, lacing a silver thread through their branches. He tipped and soared, speeding up against the dark sky and then circling back down to earth, sewing the forest to the stars above.

Gyr's heart burned. He watched Gyrfalcon's beauty and he felt afraid. He understood that he was responsible for the bird, that he alone was the keeper of its freedom to fly. He watched the bird dart and glide. He saw the same beauty he had seen in the Fianna, and he knew he would fail it too.

The bird crested on currents of air high above the tree canopy and then it flew down and almost floated in perfect circles around Gyr. The overwhelming sense that he would fail this creature pierced him and he put down his bottle and stood up, waving his arms to shoo the bird.

'Go away!' Gyr shouted. 'Go away! I can't look after you,' he yelled, his hurt swelling and expanding with Gyrfalcon's majesty. He bent down and picked up a stick from the forest floor. 'Go away!' he screamed, hurling the stick towards the bird. Gyrfalcon circled higher and dived in an elliptical arc over Gyr's head. Again, Gyr bent and gathered ammunition. He hurled sticks at the bird. 'Leave me alone, I can't look after you,' he shouted, aiming once more at Gyrfalcon who at last flew away, up through the tree canopy, his white wings cutting the air like a blade as he disappeared into the night.

Gyr's whole body was shaking as he came back to where he'd left his glass bottle. He felt such a blind confusion of rage and sorrow that he lay on the ground, looking up at the stars, his breath coming in fierce angry gasps.

To stop the million thoughts that pounded against his skull, Gyr put the cold glass of the bottle to his forehead. It cooled his skin. He could sense the liquid moving in the bottle and it soothed him. He let it balance there, spreading out his arms and legs until he lay star-shaped on the dry earth.

He thought again of Old Mahoney who'd first owned the bottle. Why had he kept poison? For rats? For foxes, maybe? Perhaps he had left down poisoned meat for stray dogs who might worry his sheep. With that thought an icy, sharp idea penetrated Gyr, moving stealthily through him. What if *he* left down poisoned meat? What if he poisoned Gyrfalcon so that its beautiful wings and noble head would hang limp and powerless forever? He could bury the bird then and be free of the painful responsibility for its flight.

Gyr lay in the silvery darkness of the forest and closed his eyes, enjoying the delicious coolness of the poison bottle against his forehead. He stretched his hands and feet, spreading himself further and further until he realised he must look like a strange imitation of the star altar in the Standing Ceremony. He thought of the elements of his life that his star altar represented: Earth, Fire, Air, Water and Spirit – Spirit whose wicker arm in the altar had been empty, now, for Gyr, held a small corked bottle of poison. He wondered if Gyrfalcon, wherever the bird was, would be able to look down and see the two stars. Would the bird be able to tell the difference between them?

A dense shadow fell across his face, and Gyr sensed someone squat down beside him.

'You wouldn't be the first warrior to falter at the Standing Ceremony,' Finn said. 'You wouldn't be the first to go up before your time, Gyr, and you wouldn't be the first to dislike what the Spirits had to say.'

Gyr scrambled up to a sitting position. The bottle fell from his forehead and Finn picked it up.

'What do you have here, Gyr?' Finn asked, but there was a mocking note to his voice that told Gyr he already knew.

Gyr scowled uneasily. 'Power,' he said.

Finn nodded his head. 'Like the knife?'

'Like the knife,' Gyr answered. 'Only this is certain power. It's not muddled, it's not about choosing. It's just definite power.'

'Remember Gyr, the poison, like the knife, is just an extension of the warrior. Your power can be definite and clear too. But would you give allegiance to such a dark liquid?'

Gyr scoffed inwardly. Typical Finn, with his wordy notions, to end up calling a clear fluid, a dark liquid. Then Gyr's heart sank and he realised he was being judgemental and full of negativity, just as the Spirit of the Future had described him. Finn had come to find him, he had even called him a warrior and said he'd not been the first person to falter at the Standing Ceremony. But Gyr didn't think he'd faltered. He believed he had failed. He had failed Finn and the Fianna, and Mum and Poppy, and perhaps he'd even failed Dad, too. He brought his hands up to his face and let tears flow freely behind them.

'What did they say to you that was so bad, Gyr?' Finn asked softly.

Gyr sobbed and his mind ran over the events of the Standing Ceremony, the impossible questions and the strange, silent masks he'd sat before. Suddenly he felt like a much younger boy, a boy who didn't understand. He felt Finn's close presence. He was physically close, as close as Gyr had been to his father that day in his special place. Gyr shook with a terrible fear that at any minute Finn would get up and run away from him as he had run from his father. But Finn did not move.

'I don't understand,' Gyr began, 'the Spirit of the Ancestors, it just repeated "Who are your people?" over and over, even when I explained who they were.'

Finn smiled, Gyr could see his teeth glinting in the dark. 'Stand up,' he ordered. Reluctantly, wiping away his tears, Gyr got to his feet and Finn said, 'Take a step forward.' Gyr took a small, awkward, faltering step into the dark.

'Who came with you?' Finn asked.

'Who came with me?' Gyr repeated. 'No one ... I mean, you're here, but you didn't move. I ... I stepped alone.'

'Did you really, Gyr? Do you not know that every time you lift your foot, every time you step forward, your ancestors and your soul-tribe are with you? If the Spirit of the Ancestors asked "Who are your people?" over and over, it is because you never answered the question. Who are your people, Gyr?'

'They're city people, business people,' Gyr said uselessly.

'Who were your great grandparents, and your great great grandparents? Who? Are you not their dream? Are you not a child that was dreamed of long ago? A thought that was kept alive through generations? The Spirits of your ancestors walk with you at every step. You must learn to speak with them for they are guides.'

'Like ghosts?' Gyr asked.

'No!' Finn roared into the night. 'Not ghosts. They are Spirits. They walk with you, and yet you Gyr, you *choose* to walk alone.'

Gyr struggled to grasp what Finn was saying. 'But, if they're dead, how can I get to know them?'

'Go home, ask your mother, ask your father. Ask who are their people? Ask the Spirits themselves. They'll tell you, if you are still enough to listen. And you must also ask yourself, who are your people in your own time? Who are your soul-tribe?'

'I don't know, you mean like the Fianna? I'd like the Fianna to be my tribe.'

'Gyr,' Finn said, laying his hand on Gyr's arm, 'you cannot join the Fianna because you belong in a different time. But know that the Fianna are in everyone. Everyone in your time has a sleeping Fianna warrior here in their breast,' he said, placing his hand over Gyr's heart. 'We never know which secret medicine will awaken them.'

Gyr looked puzzled and unsure. For a moment he found himself imagining the beautiful Fianna warriors he had seen, curled up and asleep in the hearts of his friends and family. He thought of Poppy who might have a storyteller, or a poet in her breast, and of Mum who could have a woman with a baby and a bow and arrow. Perhaps in Luke's heart there was a warrior like the boy who'd won the horse race. Suddenly, Gyr desperately wanted to be back amongst his people, blowing one of the deep Fianna horns to awaken and call forth the slumbering warriors of his own time.

He stood up, almost ready to head home to his people, but then he paused and looked at Finn. 'The Spirit of the Future said my heart was full of judgement,' he ventured.

'So it is. You will change. You were born into an age of judgement Gyr, but you can change. When the Caller calls, you will be ready.'

Gyr smiled and breathed a long, deep breath. Finn turned to him and held out the small bottle of poison.

'This is yours, Gyr. You will know what to do with it. We must be getting back. I'll walk you to my horse.'

They walked back towards the cathedral, but skirted around it to where Finn's horse was tethered. Finn lifted Gyr up onto his mare's broad back.

'You'll be all right,' he said. 'Send her home to me when you're done.'

'Finn,' Gyr said, as Finn turned the horse, 'that day ... the day Dad left ... and I looked for you everywhere ... I wanted your help, but you didn't come.'

Finn looked up into Gyr's face with such kindness and love that Gyr felt he really was one of Finn's warriors.

'Before we are born into our lives here on Earth, the gods and goddesses give us the strength and courage we will need to face everything we meet here. We forget that. So they have to remind us. If we are alone and we need help but none comes, it is because the Spirits want us to remember that they have already given us the strengths we need. It is their way, Gyr.'

Gyr managed a weak smile. He wasn't sure that he had the strength and courage he needed, but for now he would just have to trust that Finn was right.

'Goodbye Gyr,' Finn smiled.

'Finn, I didn't tell the Spirits what I stand for,' Gyr said suddenly.

'Do you know?' Finn asked, surprised.

Gyr shook his head, 'No.'

'You will, Gyr, you will,' Finn said, patting the horse to send her racing down the mountain.

Chapter Nineteen

COMING HOME

The horse knew the way. Gyr bent forward, clinging to her mane. They descended the mountain, galloping through the trees, all the way down to the gate by the reservoir. There Gyr jumped to the ground. He gave the horse a rub, stroked its fine head and said, 'Thank you, go on then, back to Finn.'

The horse galloped off and Gyr listened as its hooves pounded away into the dark. He half walked, half ran back down the little boreen. It was very dark. There was no moon here now and he could not guess what time it was. He remembered the evening when he, Poppy and Mum had walked through the dark field down to Old Mahoney's and they had all been so scared. Now he wasn't afraid. He wasn't afraid of anything, he glowed with an inner security because Finn had called him a warrior, and all through his journey down the mountain the words had sewn themselves into the lining of his heart.

He knew Mum must be worried about him and he hurried back towards the house, struck with an urgent need to let her know that everything was all right. He clattered into the yard and found Mum sitting in a crumpled heap by the front door. She was silhouetted by the light from the porch behind her, and in her big overcoat she looked strangely small and child-like. Ash lay at her feet and when he heard Gyr's step he stood up and barked furiously.

Gyr ran into Mum's outstretched arms.

'I'm sorry, I'm sorry,' he shouted.

Mum held him tight against her and Gyr could tell from her wet cheek and her breath, which came in gasps, that she had been crying.

'I was so afraid,' she whispered. 'It's so late. Poppy's been asleep for hours. We looked everywhere for you. I found your row of bottles out the back of Mr Mahoney's. I was so worried when I couldn't find you. You just disappeared.'

'I was with Finn.'

'Finn, I know, of course, but I didn't know where, or when. I didn't know if you'd come back.'

'I'm sorry Mum, I didn't mean to worry you. It was the Standing Ceremony. It was ... important.'

Mum nodded. She looked at her son, at his bright, shining eyes and open face and fresh tears fell down her cheeks. She drew him further into her arms.

'Oh Gyr. It wasn't a good day today. The doctor rang me to say Mr Mahoney died this morning. It really upset me. I mean ... I hardly knew him, but he was our neighbour. And he had no one with him. He was alone.'

Gyr felt like bursting out with everything that Finn had just said to him about never being alone, but he sensed it wasn't the right time. He sat beside Mum on the front step and held her hand. Ash came up and licked Mum's fingers. She patted his head and tried to make him sit down calmly, but he was too excited and too eager to please.

'After I'd heard about Mr Mahoney, I spent hours on the phone trying to track down his missing son. In the end I did manage to find him, only to discover he'd already left for Ireland, but when I'd finished, I realised my own child was missing. I just felt so alone,' Mum said, her voice barely a whisper. 'I know Mr Mahoney had been in the hospital, he hadn't actually been here for days, but that was different. Being dead, it's so final. Him gone, Dad gone, you gone. I felt so alone.'

'Finn says we're never alone, Mum,' Gyr tried quietly. 'Finn says the Spirits are always with us.'

Mum smiled a funny, lopsided, half-crying sort of smile. 'I know that, I do know that, but I forget. I was so worried about you and there was no one to help.'

A silence grew up around them and Ash settled down at last. After a while Gyr whispered, 'Finn says, if we're alone and need help but none comes, it's because the gods and goddesses want us to remember that they gave us the courage we need for this life before we ever came into it.'

'Does Finn say that?' Mum said, looking at Gyr's hopeful face. She smiled and squeezed his hand. 'You're cold. Let's go in and have some hot chocolate.'

They sat by the fire, drinking from steaming mugs, and Gyr told Mum all about the Standing Ceremony. He even told her everything the Spirit of the Future had said and Mum just nodded and smiled. Deliberately, he said nothing about the poison bottle. Here, in Mum's bright, warm kitchen, he couldn't understand how he had felt so very different in the shadowy forest. He knew in those moments of desperation he had nearly given his power to the dark liquid.

At last, when Gyr had finished talking, Mum got up and moved to the stove.

'Do you want some more hot chocolate, Gyr? There's some left in the saucepan.'

Gyr looked into his cup, he had drunk most of it.

'No, you have that Mum,' he said, smiling at her. 'There's loads left here.'

Chapter Twenty

THREE WATERS MEET

Gyr woke the next morning with the thought that he should go up the mountain. It echoed in his head like a call, as if somebody high in the heather were saying his name. He didn't feel it was something he could ignore; he was beginning to trust these instincts. He knew that he must go up and he knew he must bring the poison bottle with him. Carefully, he put it in his pocket. He didn't think about taking Ash. The dog's antics distracted him and today Gyr wanted the silence and space of the mountain to untangle the cat's cradle of his thoughts.

Mum had got herself involved in organising Old Mahoney's funeral, which was tomorrow, and Poppy was practising the tin whistle, murdering music. The house was unbearable. It was easy for Gyr to leave quietly and slip up the boreen, heading towards the mountain. He walked out into the blustery grey day, hoping the wind would help blow through his mind and clear his head. He climbed up past the reservoir, drawn to Three Waters Meet.

Gyr needed to understand the Standing Ceremony. He

now felt some comprehension and excitement about the idea of who his people were, and he understood all too well the painful comments with which the Spirit of the Future had branded his judgemental nature, but he still couldn't yet fathom what he stood for. Even if Finn said it didn't matter, that a warrior need only know by the time they were eighteen, Gyr still felt restless and impatient with himself for not knowing.

He walked along on the top of the bank of the Lingaun, watching how the water flowed so steadily downhill. He could tell it hadn't rained much in the last few days, for the Lingaun ran quietly. By the time he reached Three Waters Meet, he expected the three gullies to be empty, but a slow, steady trickle ran in each of the three channels. Gyr thought it only needed one fall of heavy rain and the streams would become furious torrents once more. He liked that idea, that a place could be so extreme and changeable and full of possibility.

For a while he stood looking around him, the three channels rose away on all sides. He looked to his right where one of the small streams had its source. He knew that if he followed that stream upwards he'd come to a place where he could see the Irish Sea in the far distance. That made him think of his father across in England. How far away he seemed now. How utterly unreachable. Gyr remembered the day in his special place and how his Dad had been so close to him. Suddenly Gyr couldn't understand why he had run away from his father. Why hadn't he held on to him when he had the chance?

Gyr turned around and looked to the stream that lay to his left, slipping down behind him. He knew if he went that way he'd come up on a ridge high above the house at Glenas-keogh. From there he'd be able to look down on the whole valley and see the village with its school and church and shops.

Finally, Gyr looked up at the central stream of the Lingaun. The channel wound its way higher and higher into the mountain. Up there was the forest and the deer. Gyr wondered about prince stag, had his time yet come to lead the herd? Up there were the trees and probably Finn. Up there was a landscape suitable for Gyrfalcon.

Where Gyr stood, at the place the three streams met, there was a wider, flatter area, smooth like a platform. Here, beside the pool, where the waters mixed before they hurried on downhill, this was the place.

Gyr drew the bottle from his pocket and set it gently to one side. Then, with the sharpest rock he could find, he dug a hole in the earth. The soil was stony so it was easy to carve a hole by dislodging the small stones in the ground. At last, when Gyr had gouged a hole deep enough that he could put his arm in up to his elbow, he placed the bottle at the bottom of the pit. Carefully, he laid soil over the top and placed the small stones back into the hole until the ground was level again and it was hard to see where he had buried the poison.

Then Gyr knelt by the stream and washed his hands. He watched the dirt dissolve away as it mingled with the tiny white bubbles on the water's surface and was swept up in the growing stream that hurried down the mountain towards the river and out to the forgiving sea.

Gyr stood up, knowing he had finished his task. He wasn't sure what to do now. He looked again at the three possible directions and wondered which he should follow. Perhaps he should just go home and offer to help Mum, on such a busy day she might be glad to have him there. He looked up at the central stream path one last time. Gyr knew that he really wanted to find Gyrfalcon. He decided to head that way.

Gyr scrambled into the first empty plunge pool that the water of wilder days had eked out. He went slowly, rummaging amongst the broken rocks at the bottom of the shallow basin. Mostly the stones were the deep purple and bright brown of sandstone, but occasionally his hands turned over white crystalline lumps of quartz.

In front of him there was another particularly deep plunge pool, with a steep grey rock wall at its back. The grey rock shimmered slightly, looked slippery and dangerous. Gyr hovered, uncertain, still thinking about Mum, and then he went towards the rock with a desire to climb. His hands slid and his feet scuffled, looking for stable footing. He pulled himself up the back wall of the pool, gripping with white knuckles, his head reaching level with the next rocky basin, when suddenly he came face to face with the empty staring eyes of a bleached-white sheep skull. Its teeth pointed up jaggedly out of hollow jaws. Gyr recoiled and slipped, tumbling backwards into an awkward fall. His hands scraped against the sharp rock and his legs twisted and buckled underneath him as he landed with a dull painful thud.

Chapter Twenty-One

TONY MAHONEY

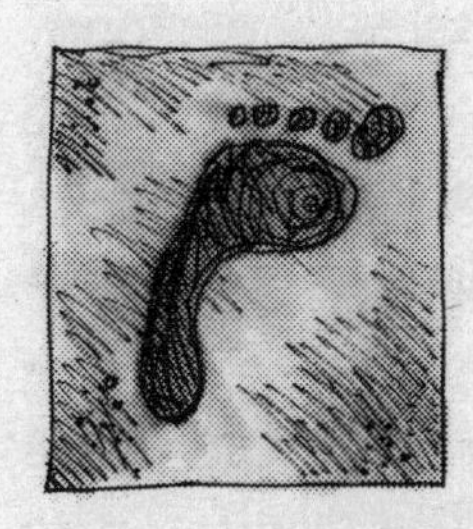

Gyr could barely comprehend how, in a matter of seconds, he had gone from feeling almost invincible to this useless, wounded state. He could barely move. Everything hurt. He had scraped every part of exposed skin, even his face. Where he had hit the ground his body groaned, but it was his left ankle that screamed with such pain that Gyr found himself absurdly biting on his hand to relieve the feeling in his foot.

He didn't feel able to stand. His head spun and all he could think of was how home was a long way off. He lay there, motionless, staring at the moss and lichen, feeling himself shrunk to a small world of short grass, sheep droppings and stone. After a time the shock of falling passed and he sat up. He tested his legs and found a way to inch forward if he stayed sitting down, pulling himself along with his hands and the one good leg that didn't ache.

Gyr didn't feel fearful, he was more angry with himself than anything else, but every so often he would feel a panic rising: what if it started to rain and he were trapped there in the flooding ravine. He tried to push these thoughts away and concentrate on moving downwards, away from Three Waters Meet, sliding and inching his way over the rough terrain. It was a huge relief when he came to a dip in the gully and saw a pony-tailed figure hunkered down by the running water. Finn! But then Gyr realised that the man's shoulders were too narrow and his frame altogether too light – it couldn't be Finn. Gyr wasn't sure if it was right to call out to this stranger for help, but he didn't really feel he had a choice.

'Well!' he shouted, inwardly laughing at this local expression of greeting.

'Well!' the man shouted back up at him, and then seeing that Gyr obviously wasn't well at all, he climbed up towards him.

Gyr watched the man, observing his long hair and long limbs that were easy and comfortable in their climb.

'Fall, did you?' the stranger said, coming close enough for Gyr to see he had an open, honest face, brown and tanned, with strong blue eyes. 'Need help?'

Gyr nodded. 'It's my ankle. I don't think I can stand.'

'I'm Tony,' the man said, dropping down and kneeling at Gyr's foot. He pulled off the shoe and peeled back Gyr's sock, feeling the ankle expertly. 'Nothing broken at least. I'm Tony Mahoney. Who are you?' he asked, sitting down beside Gyr.

Gyr weakened. The last thing he felt like right now was having to explain his name. 'I'm sorry about your Dad,' he said instead. 'We live next door. I'm Gyr.'

'Gyr? Strange name. Like the bird, gyrfalcon?' Tony asked and Gyr nodded with relief. 'I'm into rare birds, rare things generally, I suppose. I reared a kestrel once. My Dad found it. It had fallen out of a tree.'

'Did you?' Gyr asked, interested. 'Bet that was good. I've seen birds of prey up here sometimes, but I never know if they're hawks, or kestrels, or what.'

'You'll have to learn. I've a book I'll lend you,' Tony said.

'I've read about gyrfalcons,' Gyr told him, 'they can fly up to two hundred miles an hour. They're an endangered species now.'

'Like half the plant and animal life on this planet. Human beings, too, if we don't do something, and you most of all Mr Gyr. If we don't get you off this mountain, *you'll* be endangered,' he laughed.

Tony stood up and offered Gyr a hand. 'I can't carry you, I'm afraid,' he said.

Gyr stood awkwardly. As he put his foot onto the ground, his ankle screamed again and he folded up against Tony. They could only walk very slowly, one step at a time, Gyr drawing his breath sharply with each movement. Tony talked, trying to take Gyr's mind off the pain.

'I'd forgotten how green Ireland is. I haven't been here for years.'

'Where have you been then?' Gyr asked, remembering Mum's struggle to locate the missing Mahoney.

'India, South America. The last few years I've been working with street children, trying to set up schools, places where they can learn to read and write. I was in India before I came home. Before that I was in South America. Before that, Australia. That was different. I worked in the bush with the Aborigine people. They let me live with them. We went walkabout, into the dreamtime. I learned a lot from them. You know, they leave boys your age out in the bush. They have to survive on their own and find their way back to their people. The Native Americans did the same thing. They initiated their braves by leaving them out in the wild. I wonder how well you would do?' he said laughing.

Gyr said nothing. He didn't want to speak about what he knew of initiations and ceremonies, however kind Tony appeared to be, Gyr wasn't ready to trust him with everything about Finn and the Fianna.

'Where do you live, when you're in India?' he asked, carefully steering the subject away from initiations.

'I have a room behind the school.'

'Don't you have your own house?'

'No, I only need a room. That's how all the teachers live. There's a group of us there, living like that. We're lucky, most of the local families have to cram six or seven children together in one room.'

'Don't you want your own home, though?' Gyr asked

'I don't think that's important,' Tony shrugged. 'I've always travelled. I've always had a place to stay and food to eat. I don't think we need much in the way of possessions. I've never needed to have my own home.'

'But now your father's dead you'll have his,' Gyr said and then he realised that might sound rude. 'Sorry! I didn't mean–' he began, but Tony smiled and waved away Gyr's words.

'I don't plan on staying, Gyr. I want to get back to the school. Dad's place isn't important to me. Sure, I want to tidy the house up and everything, but then I'll probably rent it out.' He looked down at Gyr, 'I think the only place you really need to be at home is in your own skin.'

Chapter Twenty-Two

ORANGE

When they finally reached the farmhouse, Poppy answered the door.

'Mum,' she yelled, 'Pants-on-Fire and Finn MacCool have come for tea.'

Poppy turned to Gyr and said in a haughty tone, 'You're in trouble Pants-on-Fire, Mum is really cross that you haven't been here to help.'

Gyr blushed and scowled at Poppy as Mum appeared, looking flustered and anxious. She frowned at Gyr and for a moment she looked angry, as if she already had enough to cope with without this new problem.

'This is Tony Mahoney, Mum. He rescued me,' Gyr said quickly.

'Nice to meet you,' Tony said, extending a hand that Mum shook only after she had wiped her own on her trousers.

'Sorry, wet hands. We were about to eat. Good thing you got home in time, Gyr,' she said sarcastically. She looked at Gyr and saw him grimace in pain, she looked at Tony as he stood on the doorstep with his arm around Gyr's shoulder. Suddenly her whole face relaxed and she smiled.

'If it's not one thing, it's another,' she said, rolling her eyes and laughing. 'I'm Claire, nice to meet you too, Tony. Why not come in and eat with us, there's plenty.'

Tony gratefully accepted and followed Mum into the house. She led Gyr to the soft chair by the fire.

'Make way for the wounded,' she laughed. 'Lay an extra place at the table, would you Poppy.'

'Just *one* place? Didn't you bring the Fianna with you Mister?' Poppy asked cheekily.

'Knock it off Poppy, this is Tony from next door,' Gyr said gruffly, but Poppy wasn't put off.

'Tony Baloney from next door,' she sang.

'Well, what happened?' Mum asked, unrolling Gyr's sock.

'I just slipped. Tony found me.'

'Tony Baloney from next door, rescued Gyr when he fell on the floor,' Poppy sang, banging the cutlery drawer closed and looking up to see if Tony was watching her.

'I don't think it's serious,' Tony said, winking at Poppy.

'It seems fine to me, just a sprain. But you'll have to rest it,' Mum agreed.

'Tony Baloney from next door, thought Gyr's leg wasn't sore,' Poppy chimed.

'Ah now, I didn't say that. I said it's not serious. I'm sure it's sore,' Tony added as Gyr winced at the cold witch hazel Mum was dabbing on his ankle.

'Nothing rhymes with serious though, does it?' Gyr grumbled at his sister.

'Mister Serious, he's imperious!' Poppy stuck out her tongue. 'See!'

'I bet you don't know what imperious means,' taunted Gyr.

'I do,' said Poppy, pouting.

'Tell me then.'

'No. I don't want to.'

'Ha,' said Gyr, 'I knew you couldn't.'

'I can,' shouted Poppy.

Mum's voice rose over their argument. 'That's enough, both of you!'

Gyr and Poppy grinned at each other.

Mum fed Gyr arnica and held her hand up to his cheek to give it a gentle rub. 'You'll mend. Now, let's eat.'

'Tony Mahoney wants macaroni,' Poppy sang, sitting at the table and pulling out the chair next to her. 'Come and sit here, Mister Macaroni,' she instructed.

'You know Poppy, I hate to disappoint you, but we're Mah-knees. You spell it Mahoney, but you say Mah-knee. Mah-knee and macaroni don't rhyme.'

'Oh, that's my fault, I'm afraid,' Mum interrupted. 'I always say Mahoney, like baloney. The English version, I guess. Sit down anyway Tony, you must be hungry after all your rescuing. Poppy won't bite, she'll just turn everything you say into a rhyme.'

'Everything?' Tony questioned.

'Ring a ding ding!' Poppy sang.

'Most people get the runs, Poppy has the rhymes!' Gyr snorted.

'Gyr! Not at the table,' Mum frowned. 'Sorry Tony, they're not this bad normally, this must be a special performance just for you,' she said, bringing over the food.

'Orange,' Tony said.

'Orange?' Gyr and Poppy echoed.

'Orange, Miss Poet. If you're a real poet then by the end of this meal you'll find me a word that rhymes with orange.'

'Porange,' Poppy replied at once.

'That the best you can do?'

'Forange!'

Tony slowly shook his head. Poppy pursed her lips and fell silent.

Mum and Tony talked about the funeral arrangements for the following day and about Mr Mahoney's last days in the hospital. Tony was very grateful for all that Mum had done for his father. They talked about Old Mahoney's life and then their conversation turned to other, more distant neighbours. Who was who, who had lived in the few tumble- down cottages that were scattered along the mountain road. They talked about how life had been so different when Tony was young, how there had been few tractors, or cars, or even telephones. Every so often, Poppy interrupted with something she hoped rhymed with orange, but she couldn't find anything that was a real word.

Tony remembered a story from his own childhood of a bad winter when it had snowed for two weeks solid and the mountain road had been completely cut off from the village.

'Everyday for two weeks the mountain people shovelled snow to clear a path downhill and the villagers shovelled snow to clear a path uphill. They kept at it all day long, day in, day out, until at last they could see each other in the distance, and they knew that the next day they would break through and finally get supplies to the mountain people.' Tony hesitated and paused for effect.

'And?' Gyr asked.

'And then that night, it poured with rain. When they woke in the morning there wasn't a snowflake to be seen!'

Mum and Poppy laughed, but Gyr scowled.

'That's not funny!' he said.

'You're right Gyr, it's not funny,' Tony admitted. 'They didn't have a lot in those days, everything they had came from what they could create with their own two hands. To spend two weeks digging snow and then have it rain, that wasn't funny at all, but they were used to that kind of thing, they were heroic people.'

'What do you think is heroic now, in our time, Tony? What do you think a hero should stand for these days?' Gyr asked.

Tony scratched his nose.

'Well,' he said thoughtfully, 'maybe to stand up for the truth when no one else is. I've seen a lot of corruption across the world. I think it's important to stand for truth. But you also need to stand for your own truth. You have to be yourself, who you really are at the deepest level. If you don't stand for that, you'll never really learn to stand for anything else.'

Gyr nodded, questions tumbling into his mind. Mum got up and began to clear the table.

'But what you stand for in life has to keep changing,' she said. 'I don't think you can just say one thing that you stand for and stay with that forever. When you're young you can stand for whatever you like, but when you get older and you have different responsibilities, like children, you have to stand for them.'

Tony got up from his chair to help Mum and Gyr got to his feet too, but his ankle hurt him and he winced.

'Sit down Gyr, rest your foot,' Mum said, putting her hands on his shoulders. 'I think the most heroic thing we can do is just be ordinary. Doing the same thing day in, day out, without complaint and with a good heart. Washing-up everyday with a smile on your face, now that's heroic.'

'Like the snow men?' Poppy asked.

'Like the snow men,' Mum said, giving the top of Poppy's head a kiss.

There was a silence in the kitchen for a moment, and then Gyr broke it. 'Like the men who long ago had to shovel lots of snow, thinking, thinking all the time, of a way to make orange rhyme.' He grinned at Poppy and she looked at him with delight.

'That was brilliant,' she said, clapping her hands, 'but I bet even you can't make orange rhyme.'

Gyr thought for a moment then shook his head.

'I can't either,' said Tony Mahoney, 'and I've been trying for years!'

Chapter Twenty-Three

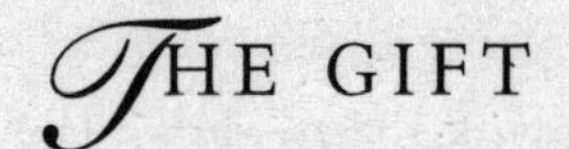

All through the following week, the air at Glenaskeogh was filled with the sounds of sawing and hammering and the smell of fresh paint as Tony went about the business of tidying Old Mahoney's cottage. The funeral had gone well. Everyone agreed that Mr Mahoney had been a grand old man who'd lived a long good life. It seemed only Gyr and Poppy remembered him as frightening and grumpy. Gyr's ankle improved and he took to going down after school to help out and potter around behind Tony. He liked Tony's amiable manner. The two of them fell quite naturally into an easy rhythm of work and conversation.

When Tony discovered the signs of Gyr having been in the bottle heap, he told him to take what he wanted, but Gyr declined. He'd gone off bottles. Instead he was happy to borrow Tony's bird book, poring over the pages on hawks and falcons. He was determined to learn how to tell them apart, but it was confusing, they mostly looked similar, only the snow-white gyrfalcons were easily identifiable.

Whenever he looked at their pictures, Gyr felt a sharp longing in his chest. He had not seen or even felt the presence of Gyrfalcon since he had driven the bird away that night in the forest. Gyr felt a terrible emptiness without Gyrfalcon.

On Saturday, Gyr woke very early. The house was quiet, Mum and Poppy were still sleeping. Gyr sat up in bed and tweaked back the curtain. It was a bright, clear day. He got out of bed and opened the window, and a soft scent came into the room on a gentle breeze. Something inviting was out there. He looked across the fields, over the tops of the greening trees and he saw the arched wings of a bird of prey skim the horizon. Hawk? Kestrel? Gyr frowned. He pressed his face against the window pane, watching the bird as it flew effortlessly along, gliding without even seeming to move its wings. He saw it land in the branches of one of the large ash trees at the bottom of the Gate Field.

'Wait for me!' Gyr whispered under his breath.

At the front door he jammed the bottoms of his pyjamas into his wellies. He crept out of the house and ran down into the field. The bird was gone. For a moment, Gyr felt silly to be up and outside in his pyjamas so early on a Saturday. Yet the morning was so alive, so thick and full with things happening, with currents of air, with birdsong and promise that he felt privileged to be there. He contemplated going down to his special place, but suddenly the bird was back, skimming the treetops, pushing west along the mountain road. Gyr followed behind the bird, which now skimmed so low to the ground Gyr felt it must surely be playing with him.

Gyr followed it to the ring fort field. The bird had

disappeared again, but Gyr didn't mind. He stood at the gate into the field and looked in. It was empty, as ever, but now the hedgerows that lined its borders were breaking into leaf and the grass, instead of being pale, winter green, was quickening with new life. Gyr climbed the gate and made his way to the ring fort. It seemed such a scrubby, sad sort of place, abandoned and brambled with no suggestion of its former glory. Gyr wondered if badgers lived there, or foxes, or rabbits, but he could find no sign of any life at all. Not quite sure what to do, he sat down, cross-legged, in the middle of the fort.

He closed his eyes. He listened. He wished. He wished for Finn and he wished for Gyrfalcon. He felt he would do anything to have the bird in his life again. Since his desperate hour in the forest he had come to realise that the bird was a secret, magical part of him that he could neither fully understand nor do without. He accepted that looking after such a creature of beauty would be a constant struggle, but now he knew he had no choice: the bird was too much a part of his being for him ever to be content without its presence.

He knew that finding a landscape for Gyrfalcon in this world might never be easy, but since he had fallen at Three Waters Meet, Gyr understood that he himself had to live in the safe landscape of Glenaskeogh. Gyr did not belong on the misted, changing moors of the mountain. Gyrfalcon might struggle in Gyr's landscape, but if he would only come back, Gyr vowed, he would protect him as well as he was able.

Over and over Gyr whispered the name Finn MacCumhail, calmly and without anger or desperation. Minutes passed and Gyr opened his eyes once more to the field. Disappointed he tried again. Stay calm, he told himself. He called for help. He called to the Spirits of his ancestors and to his people.

Finally, Gyr lay back in the fresh grass. It was cold and slightly damp. He watched a few white clouds drift over the pale blue sky above him. Then curved wings suddenly cut through the stillness of the sky overhead and, gliding into an updraft, the bird sped away across the field. A hawk, surely, Gyr thought as his body tingled. He closed his eyes and listened to the way his body thrilled at the bird's presence. When he opened his eyes again, he was looking at the timber frame of the Great Hall in the Fianna camp.

Finn was sitting cross-legged in front of Gyr, a small leather parcel lay in his lap. Gyr sat up at once, embarrassed to be lying down in front of Finn, embarrassed to be in his pyjamas. He crossed his legs in the same way as Finn, and then he beamed with the pure pleasure of being there, with Finn, beneath the rafters of the great hall. Gyr looked about him and out into the green clearing, which seemed strangely empty without the Fianna's colourful tents. The sun beat down outside and Gyr judged it must still be summer, perhaps not long after the Standing Ceremony. In the hall above their heads he could sense the echo of the swallow that had flown so smoothly from one gable-end to the other that day, shortly before the solstice.

'There's something I want to give you,' Finn said, offering the parcel. It was neatly wrapped in leather, tied by two thongs.

'For me?' Gyr asked, already burning with curiosity.

'You, Gyr, cannot cross the doorway of worlds forever, nor stay amongst us. But I sense you are ready to carry the Fianna with you.'

Finn placed the gift gently in Gyr's hands, hands that trembled as they reached forward and closed around the soft leather.

'Thank you, Finn. Thank you for everything,' Gyr said, struggling to express how much gratitude he felt, but no words could really explain his feelings. Finn was looking at him with such tenderness, and yet Gyr could sense there was something else in his look, a sorrow perhaps. 'It's not the last time, is it? Can I ... will I ... see you again?'

Finn laid his hands on Gyr's shoulders.

'If the gods and goddesses will it, I shall be there,' he said.

Gyr looked stricken. He didn't want this to be the last time, he sought for something to say, his hands clutching Finn's gift.

'What happens ... I want to know what happens when a warrior fails ... when they don't manage to stand for the things that they've been called to stand for. Are the Spirits angry?'

'The gods and goddesses are never angry with us. They forgive. If we fail their tests then they ask us to do them again. Sometimes we make the same mistake three or four times before we learn.'

'They forgive us,' Gyr whispered. 'What about the other Fianna? Do they forgive too? It can be hard, can't it?' he said, thinking of his feelings towards his dad.

'To not forgive someone is to carry a great rock through life. The longer you carry the rock, the heavier it gets. Better to put it down, travel light.'

Gyr nodded, but frowned. He wasn't sure if that was all there was to it.

'You think you are in pain, but the heaviest stone is the one your father carries for he cannot forgive himself. To not forgive ourselves is to carry a mountain on our shoulders. Gyr, put down your rock, it will help your father to forgive himself. If you don't, your rock will grow into two rocks because a time will come when you will not be able to forgive yourself for having spent a whole lifetime carrying so much weight. Under such mountains of bitterness the soul dies. The Spirits do not give us our souls so that we may crush them under such a burden.'

Gyr nodded. He felt lighter, easier, as if something really had been lifted from his heart. 'I've been thinking for a while about the questions the Spirits ask. I think I know what I stand for now,' he said.

'You don't need to tell me, Gyr. What you stand for is between you and the Spirits.'

Gyr began to open Finn's gift. 'I stand,' he said, struggling with his awkwardness and with the leather thongs on the parcel, 'I stand for my flight.' Then, accepting he must add another word, a word he had never said before, a word that tasted strange and powerful on his tongue, Gyr added, 'I stand for my soul flight.'

At last the leather thongs unfurled to reveal a beautifully crafted knife, just as fine and perfect as the one Finn wore at his waist. As Gyr looked up with shining eyes to thank Finn, he realised both Finn and the Great Hall were gone. He was just a boy, alone in a field. He looked down, turning the knife over in his hands, and he saw there, carved on the handle, the outstretched wings of a gyrfalcon.

Gyr leapt to his feet and as he did so Gyrfalcon soared up, seemingly from the ground in front of him. The bird flew into the clean morning air, his wings lifting with their natural power and grace. Gyrfalcon circled the boy in the field and for a time Gyr just stood there, watching, holding the knife in his hands.

Above his head, Gyrfalcon flew. Gliding on outstretched wings it soared high over the ring fort. Arcing upwards on a swift current it flew over the heather moors of the bare mountain. Gyrfalcon flew between all worlds. It flew between the gable-ends of Gyr's life.

Proudly holding his knife, constantly glancing down to gaze at its perfect blade, Gyr began walking home. Gyrfalcon sped on ahead of him and came briefly to rest in the special place where a thousand yellow catkins hung from the branches of the hazel trees, like tickertape at a parade. Then the bird stretched its wings once more and flew off to circle the house at Glenaskeogh. The house to which Gyr headed now, to show Mum and Poppy his gift, and to ring Dad and tell him all about it.

A Note from the Author

Dear Reader,

Thank you very much for choosing my book. I hope you enjoyed it. I wonder what you think of it? Most (but not all) of the things I put in the book are parts of my own life, as if I just took the ingredients from our kitchen cupboard, or went out and harvested them from our vegetable garden. Like 'Mum', I live with my son and daughter in an old farmhouse high up on the slopes of Sliabh na mBan, and we are all rather like the characters in this book.

Just as in the story, the mountain is a wild and untameable place. In winter we can have terrible storms and the long, dark nights can be very frightening. But it's also a beautiful place, full of magic and silence, where you can easily encounter the spirit of Finn MacCumhail, even if you don't actually meet him face to face!

I really wrote *Gyrfalcon* for my son, Sliabh, and as I wrote it I thought mainly about him, and the place we live, and the task of heroes in our own time. The book is full of the things I've experienced and the things I care about. I had a lot of fun writing it and I hope my passion for the ingredients of the story comes across to you, the reader.

My best wishes,

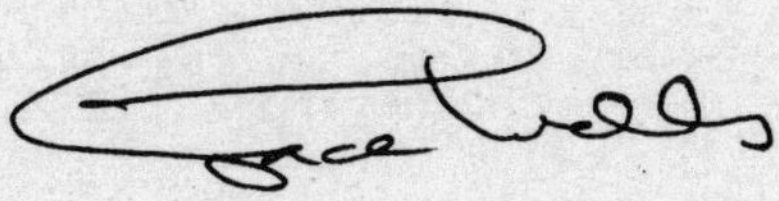